D0627406

CRASH TEST LOVE

Also by Ted Michael

The Diamonds

CRASH TEST LOVE

TED MICHAEL

DELACORTE PRESS

This is a work of fiction. Names, characters, places, and incidents either are the product of the author's imagination or are used fictitiously. Any resemblance to actual persons, living or dead, events, or locales is entirely coincidental.

Copyright © 2010 by Ted Michael

All rights reserved. Published in the United States by Delacorte Press, an imprint of Random House Children's Books, a division of Random House, Inc., New York.

Delacorte Press is a registered trademark and the colophon is a trademark of Random House, Inc.

Visit us on the Web! www.randomhouse.com/teens

Educators and librarians, for a variety of teaching tools, visit us at www.randomhouse.com/teachers

Library of Congress Cataloging-in-Publication Data is available upon request.

ISBN 978-0-385-73580-3 (tr. pbk.)
ISBN 978-0-375-89648-4 (e-book)

The text of this book is set in 11-point Cushing

Book design by Marci Senders

Printed in the United States of America

10 9 8 7 6 5 4 3 2 1

First Edition

Random House Children's Books supports the First Amendment and celebrates the right to read.

For my parents

&

for anyone who has loved,
lost,
and lived to write about it

CRASH TEST LOVE

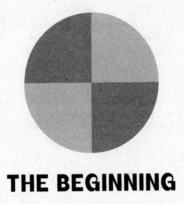

THE BEGINNING

Hearts will be practical only when they are made unbreakable.

—from *The Wizard of Oz* (1939)

HENRY

I am not the girlfriend type of guy.

I want to get it out there and be completely honest.

I am not *the girlfriend type of guy.*

I won't: hold your hand, buy you flowers, have dinner with your parents.

I will: kiss you until your legs collapse and you beg me to lift you up and start all over again.

I'm sorry if that hurts your feelings, ladies, but you should know exactly what you're getting into.

It's only fair.

INT.–BACKSEAT OF MY CAR, SATURDAY NIGHT, LABOR DAY WEEKEND

I am bored.

HER

And I was like, <u>really</u>, you like my hair like <u>this</u>? On top of my head?

ME

(blank stare)

HER

Because <u>I</u> think it looks better in braids. I know that sounds so third grade, but it's true!

ME

(blank stare)

HER

Don't you agree, Reinaldo?

ME

(even blanker stare)

HER

Reinaldo? Hel-<u>lo</u>?

I forget she is talking to me because my name is not Reinaldo. It's what I told her my name is, though, so it makes sense she's calling me that. I try to remember *her* name—Marissa? Marisol? Something with an *M*?—but I can't. I suddenly wish I hadn't suggested we leave the party to be alone in my car. It's much easier to tune some-one out in a large group. But here we are, in the back of my Jeep. I think about how many girls I've been with in this very same position. Our legs are touching, and even though it's the time I would normally make my move, I have a gnawing feeling this is *not* going to happen. Whoever this girl is sitting next to me, she seems incredi-bly . . . young. But it's still worth a shot.

HER

Did you hear a single thing I just said?

ME

Maybe you should take your dress off—it's really hot
in here.

HER

(giving me a look I don't even have to describe)
You are a pig, Reinaldo! A pig!

She slams my car door behind her as she leaves. I am slightly upset. Not because I liked her (she was boring) or because she thinks I'm a pig (I am) or even because it's pretty clear I'm not getting any tonight; I am upset because I can usually pick them pretty well. Girls, that is. I can see a girl and know within seconds what her deal is. What she likes and what she hates and whether she moans when she's being kissed. It's a talent I have. Some people are good with numbers. I am good with women.

Just not this one. The Hello Kitty hair clip should've tipped me off.

I get out of my car. It's dark, but not too dark. Even though I'm standing in the parking lot I can hear the noise coming from inside the hotel. Music. Dance music. You should know that I love to dance. *Love* to dance. Not professionally or anything, but in a club where it's loud and crazy. That's one of the reasons I dig parties. I like to have a good time. And there's nothing wrong with that—despite what anybody says.

This particular party is a Sweet Sixteen for a girl who

goes to my high school. Usually when I crash Sweet Sixteens, I like to go where no one knows me and I can pretend to be someone else entirely. I get a rush from sneaking into a party I wasn't invited to and dancing. Well, not *just* dancing. Finding a cute girl to hook up with and hopefully making a little mischief in the process. Escaping the monotony of life for a few hours. Duke and Nigel (my co-crashers) have never understood this about me, and they probably never will. They just think crashing parties is *fun*. They don't know firsthand the need to escape. To flee. To invent fake names and fake pasts and know that someone, some girl, actually believes it all. This makes me feel powerful. It also makes me kind of an asshole, but I don't really care.

This is probably why I love movies so much. The idea of transforming into an entirely different person on-screen than who you are in real life. You would think that'd make me a wannabe actor, but I'm not. I do want to study film in college, though, and write screenplays. Like Charlie Kaufman or Alan Ball or Joel and Ethan Coen. I want to *make* movies, to create something from nothing. Every day I imagine my interactions as part of one big script; I see things as if my whole existence is on film. I've been this way for a while now, and I can't imagine changing anytime soon. I want to be a writer so I can hide behind a computer or even a pen and paper and make decisions by myself. Without anyone interfering. Without anyone saying no.

Inside, it's as spectacular as a Baz Luhrmann film, only with a crowd made up entirely of horny sixteen-year-olds. The guys here look so tiny, like miniature men. Did I ever look that small? Granted, I'm not even two years older—but somehow I skipped that awkward phase of pimples and wispy mustaches.

I wasn't officially invited to this extravaganza, but since most everyone here goes to East Shore, I am known. Duke and Nigel are too (slightly less than me, but still). Truth be told, it's a pretty chill setup. The girls seem ready to party, the music is nice and hip-hoppy, and the food smells good. Not a bad way to close the summer. The fact that school is starting up again next week makes me wanna hurl, but I'm not going to think about that right now.

I head over to a table covered with a bunch of snacks, shrimp, and napkins. And mini quiches. People *love* mini quiches. This is when my buddies approach me.

DUKE is just over six feet tall with lots of brown hair. He's built, plays football, and he's pretty smart, despite talking like he's a character in a Judd Apatow flick.

NIGEL is shortish and always dressed up. He plays the cello like a pro, but Duke and I are the only ones who know he can play at all.

The three of us have been inseparable since we were twelve. We started crashing Sweet Sixteens last year, when Duke turned seventeen and got a car. (Don't judge—there's not much else to do on Long Island.) I got my cousin's hand-me-down Jeep about three months ago, on my seventeenth birthday, and now we alternate driving so we can (try to) drink.

Nigel and Duke are more talk than anything, really. They've never had girlfriends, and they usually mess things up even when they *do* get the chance to score—not that it happens often. I, on the other hand, seem to attract more girls than any person should. They cling to me like barnacles. I kind of dated someone once (the closest thing *I've* had to a girlfriend, anyway), but it was a long time ago and the relationship, if you can even call it that, ended badly. Since then, I like to fly solo.

NIGEL

Yo, Henry, how'd it go?

DUKE

Get any tail?

Only Duke would use the word *tail* in reference to women.

ME

(eating a pig in a blanket)

Not yet, gentlemen. But the night is young.

DUKE

You're cool to drive, right?

ME

I'm cool. Why, what's up?

NIGEL

(pointing to the bar a few feet away)

Look how stocked they are!

It's true. They have all the fancy stuff. The bartender, though, seems like a total bitch. I doubt she'll be lax about serving us. (Tonight, Nigel's folks—our usual suppliers— locked their liquor cabinet, so we're on our own.)

A few girls pass by and giggle. I give a little wave. They run away.

ME

You can try, dude, but it's never gonna happen.

NIGEL

I like a challenge.

DUKE

Your mom likes a challenge.

NIGEL

Shut up.

DUKE

Let's make a bet, Henry: if we can get the
bartender to serve us, then you give us each
five bucks.

ME

No.

NIGEL

Oh, come on. It's all in good fun.

ME

How about this: if you get her to serve you, you
each give _me_ five bucks for gas, seeing as how I
picked your asses up and drove you here.

NIGEL

Ha. No.

ME

Okay, how about <u>this:</u> whether you get her to serve

you or not, you'll each still give me five bucks

for gas.

DUKE

I don't like that bet.

ME

It's not a bet. I need the cash. This is my way of

telling you.

DUKE

Fine. Just don't drink, okay? You need to

drive us home.

ME

Deal.

NIGEL

Back to the bartender. I recognize her. My brother

used to date this girl named Leslie, who went to

middle school with her. I think her name is Stacy.
Or maybe Sapphire. If that's not an in, what is?

ME

You're right. She'll <u>totally</u> serve you once you
mention that.

Not.

Duke and Nigel slip away, and I am left standing alone
at the hors d'oeuvres table. This is not, in my experience,
such a bad place to be.

"What's with all the quiche?" asks a voice from behind
me.

I turn around and there is this *girl*. She looks around my
age, but the closer I examine her, the more I realize she is
not a girl. I mean, she is but she isn't. She's a *woman*. She
has dark brown hair and perfect skin. She is beautiful.

ME

Do I know you?

HER

I don't know, do you? (She picks up a mini quiche
and takes a bite. She swallows but crushes the rest
in a napkin, tossing it into the garbage.) Gross.

ME

I've never seen you before.

HER

That makes sense. I just moved here.

I cannot take my eyes off her. The way she walks is not walking. It's gliding. I can see every line and curve of her body. I want her immediately. But it's more than sexual. It's something I can't describe.

Across from us is a tiny alcove with a window overlooking the hotel grounds. She sits on the ledge.

HER

Care to join me?

I am suddenly so glad that nothing happened with whatshername in my car, because then I would not be experiencing this right now. Whatever this is.

We sit for what feels like a long time. Normally I have a routine:

1. Compliment
2. Flatter (which is similar to #1 but more over-the-top, and typically involves physical contact)
3. Get It On

It's like this: girls like when you take charge and tell them what you want. And what they want. I am great at the art of seduction (whatshername being an exception). What I am *not* great at is the follow-through. I don't hook up with the same girl more than once. It's too complicated. Too much work. Too much responsibility.

I stare at this gorgeous creature beside me and wonder what she looks like *minus* her dress and *plus* me on top of her. I begin to plan my attack.

HER

I guess you're the silent type.

ME

Not usually. But you've got me speechless.

HER

(laughing)

Oh. I see. Speechless, huh?

ME

Well. <u>Kind of</u> speechless.

HER

I bet you say that to all the girls.

ME

No. I don't.

HER

<u>Sure.</u> So what's your name, stranger?

Something about her makes me want to say *Henry Arlington.* But that is completely against the Crasher Code (which Duke, Nigel, and I follow strictly). Rule #1: *Never tell a girl your real name.* And even though I have this sudden urge to be, well, honest, I know myself. Honesty is something I will probably regret.

HER

I didn't realize that was such a hard question. (She reaches for her purse, as if she's about to leave.)

ME

Henry.

I don't know why I say it, but I do.

HER

Good name. Classic. Nice to meet you, Henry.
I'm Garrett.

Unusual, but it suits her. Garrett. She looks right at me when she says it, too, which both unnerves and exhilarates me. I feel . . . naked. (I'm not, but I could be wearing absolutely nothing and I wouldn't feel any more vulnerable than I do right now.)

Garrett crosses her legs and her dress rides up just enough to show off how amazing those legs truly are. This is about the time I'd normally say that my car is parked close by and casually mention how comfortable the backseat is. Now, though, I can't bring myself to do anything that will imply I'm less than a total gentleman.

GARRETT

So, how do you know Erica? Our dads went to grad
school together.

Erica. Erica. Who is Erica?

GARRETT

The birthday girl? (Dramatic pause.) Erica Warner?
(She looks at me skeptically.) Are you supposed to
be here?

ME

Hmm?

GARRETT

Were you invited?

ME

Depends on what you mean by invited.

GARRETT

I guess by <u>invited</u> I mean that, you know, one day
you opened your mailbox and there was a really
fancy <u>invitation</u> inside, addressed to you, <u>inviting</u>
you to come and celebrate Erica's Sweet Sixteen.

ME

Interesting.

GARRETT

So were you?

ME

Invited?

GARRETT

Yes.

ME

Absolutely not. You have great eyes. They're so . . .

GARRETT

Blue?

ME

Yeah.

GARRETT

I get that a lot.

ME

I can see why.

GARRETT

Because they're blue.

ME

Right.

I wait to see if she'll leave, but she doesn't. She smiles.

GARRETT

I feel like I know you from somewhere. (She laughs,
and the sound makes me happy. I am thankful she
does not have an annoying, Taser-worthy laugh.)
Gosh, that makes me sound crazy, doesn't it?

ME

No. I don't think so.

I've never believed in energy or vibes or any of that bullshit, but just being near this girl puts me at ease. All of a
sudden I cannot seem to stop myself from talking.

ME

Did you have a nice summer? What did you do? I
work at this little movie theater in Huntington. Do
you like movies? Where are you gonna
go to school?

GARRETT

Whoa, there! Calm down. (She puts a hand on my
knee. I know immediately this is not a sexual move,
but one of concern. Still, when she touches me,
something sparks between us.) Are you okay?

ME

Yeah, sure. I guess.

I wipe my forehead. It's dripping with sweat.

GARRETT

You don't look so great, Henry. Let me get you
some water.

At the same time she gets up, Duke and Nigel practically crash into me. They're both breathing hard and their eyes are everywhere.

NIGEL

We gotta go, dude.

ME

What?

DUKE

That bartender. Man. We gotta peace.

ME

What happened?

DUKE

(looking behind him)

Can we talk about it later? Like, when we're far, far

away from here?

NIGEL

It's a sixty-nine, Henry. <u>A sixty-nine.</u> With booze.

I stand up immediately. A sixty-nine with booze is Crasher Code for getting caught stealing alcohol. (We call every emergency a sixty-nine with [fill in the blank] because, you know, it's funny.) Normally, I'd have no problem getting the hell out of here with D & N, but I think of Garrett and realize I don't want to leave. I consider tossing the keys to Duke and letting him drive my car home.

DUKE

Dude, <u>what</u> is your <u>problem</u>? Let's go!

If I tell them I want to stay, I'll have to explain that it's because of Garrett. And if I want to stay because of Garrett, they'll assume it's because I want to Get Freaky with her, and one of the cardinal rules of the Crasher Code is *No hos before bros*. I could attempt to explain that I have never felt such an immediate connection with anyone in my entire life, but that would make me sound like a total loser *and* it would be against both the Crasher Code (punishable by death or, at least, social genocide) and my own personal code: No Girlfriends. Ever.

Suddenly, Garrett is back, holding out a glass of water for me. She acknowledges Duke and Nigel with curiosity.

GARRETT
Is everything all right?

I debate whether to ask for her phone number. How can I pull that off with Duke and Nigel standing right here? I suddenly wish they would just go away. Vanish. Garrett looks genuinely concerned; I am not sure how that makes me feel.

DUKE
Well, hello there, my dear. My name is Charlie von Huseldorf and I come from money. Oil money. What's your name?

GARRETT
What?

Then we hear a voice. "That's them, over there!" We turn and see the bartender coming toward us with two security guards. *Big* security guards. They do not look happy.

NIGEL
(grabbing my arm)
Now!

ME
(to Garrett)
I'm sorry. I've gotta go.

GARRETT
But—

DUKE
Later, sexy!

We run out of the hotel lobby and into the parking lot. I don't hear anyone following us, but I also don't turn around to look. I spot my car and click it open. We pile inside.

NIGEL
Man! That was close.

DUKE

Nice going, douche monster. It was all your

fault anyway.

NIGEL

It definitely was <u>not</u> my fault. It was yours!

DUKE

Maybe it was your mom's fault.

NIGEL

Shut up.

I start the engine. Duke selects a synthy electropop album we all love, Owl City's *Maybe I'm Dreaming*, and rolls
down the windows until the air-conditioning kicks in.

We drive for a few minutes until our breathing is steady.
Then the inevitable questioning begins.

NIGEL

So . . . who was the chick? She was hot.

DUKE

Really hot. I'd bang her.

NIGEL

You're not exactly picky.

DUKE

Well, I wouldn't bang your mom.

NIGEL

Ouch.

DUKE

That's what she said. Last night. When I
banged her.

NIGEL

Lame, dude. Lame.

DUKE

(to me)

What did you tell her your name was?

ME

I forget.

DUKE

Shut up. You're not gonna tell us?

ME

It's not important.

NIGEL

It's <u>totally</u> important! What's with you?

ME

I dunno. I just feel weird.

DUKE

At least answer us this: did you guys fool around?

I should just say no. I mean, nothing happened. But I feel so strange about the whole thing that I remain silent.

DUKE

I knew it! Dude. We want <u>details,</u> my man. Details.

NIGEL

All in good time, Duke. (He leans forward to pat my shoulder. Nigel knows when not to press an issue—a skill Duke most definitely lacks.) Henry will tell us when he's ready. Right, Enrico?

I ignore the question. I cannot stop thinking about Garrett. There has only been one person in my entire life who, even though she's gone, I think about constantly: my mother. I haven't seen her in five years. As I get lost in the music and the speed of my car on the highway, I wonder if Garrett will be the second woman who will leave me and never look back.

GARRETT

IF I weren't so self-conscious, I could probably get ready very quickly in the morning.

But the truth is that I'm an emotional *mess*. It takes me practically an entire hour just to figure out what I'm going to wear, let alone do my makeup, fix my hair, and stare at myself in the mirror (and suck in my stomach and my cheeks and make sure my butt looks good). Getting ready in the morning is never easy, but it's especially tough when you're starting a brand-new high school *senior year* on Long Island, where the girls are notorious bitches and the guys all look like Abercrombie models.

Neurotic is not the image I project, of course. If you were to meet me on the street, I would go out of my way to be casual and cool, to make you think I'm one of those girls who doesn't care about how she looks and wants people to judge her on her *personality.* Whatever that means.

So now you know one of my (many) secrets: I am insecure. Welcome to my life.

"No time for pictures!" I yell, tramping down the stairs, grabbing my bag, and heading straight for my car.

"Now, listen to me, young lady," my father says, standing at the breakfast island (yes, our new kitchen has a breakfast island) and frowning. "I've taken a picture of you on your first day of school for the past . . . however many years, and I'm certainly not going to miss this one." Dad holds up his digital camera. "It'll only take five minutes."

I know from experience it will be less painful to let him take the picture than to argue. "Fine," I say. "But just one."

Dad leads me outside. At our old town house in Chicago, the house I'd lived in for my entire life in the city that I love, there was a spot right by the front door where we took First Day of School photos. Here, though, in this completely new place, this entirely foreign world, the possibilities are endless.

"Where would you like to stand, darling?"

I look around, overwhelmed by the sheer amount of grass and trees. Suburbia. "I don't care. Just take it, please. I'm gonna be late."

"Here, in front of the hydrangea? No, no. Maybe there, by the car? We don't want the neighbors' house in the picture, though. That orange color is just wacky."

When my father was hired to head up the film department at Columbia, I was happy for him. Really. But I never thought he'd have the balls to leave his job at U Chicago. It was the biggest surprise of my life to learn that we were actually moving, that I was going to a new school—a *public* school—for senior year. That was less than two months ago. I'm still in shock.

"Yoo-hoo!" comes a voice from the side of the house. "I didn't miss the photo shoot, did I?"

My mother prances into view, a watering can in one hand and a sprinkled donut in the other. She's wearing a pair of overalls with patches everywhere that say things like *Peace* and *Harmony*. "Garrett, you look beautiful! What a great way to begin the best year of your life!"

My mother is a natural optimist, a trait I find both

annoying and (recently) admirable. She knows I'm pissed I have to spend senior year with *no* friends, and she's gone a little overboard trying to reassure me that everything will work out "Just Fine" (Mary J. Blige, 2007). I already know it won't, though, so the whole charade is pointless.

I roll my eyes. "Are we done yet?"

"Garrett, put your right hand on your right hip," Mom instructs, "and the other on your left leg."

"No."

"Oh, come on! That's what all the models do."

"No, Mom, it's not."

"Yes it is." She places the watering can on the ground and finishes the donut in one bite. Then she poses. "Do it like me."

"You are insane," I say, trying not to laugh. "Dad, please just take the picture."

"Okay, okay," he says, steadying the camera. I smile. "There we go. Gorgeous."

"I seriously doubt that." I get into my car (the only good thing that has come from moving to Long Island so far) and close the door. My mother calls my name. "Yes?" I say through the window.

"Good luck, honey," she says, kissing the glass. "We love you."

I don't respond. By the time I leave our neighborhood, I have exactly twenty minutes to get to school.

East Shore is bigger than Mercer, my last high school. The outside is covered with bricks, the inside in beige paint. There are tons of windows and hallways that seem never-ending.

I arrive about half an hour early. I'm nervous. The dean introduces himself and prints out a copy of my schedule. A freckled girl who looks like she could've been in one of the Gremlins movies is instructed to show me around. We're barely outside the dean's office when she tells me she was named after Marilyn Monroe. "People say I remind them of her all the time," Marilyn says, motioning for me to follow. "Minus my limp. We have very similar demeanors."

We stroll toward what I assume is the senior hallway. "Where are you from again?" she asks.

"Chicago."

She nods. "The Windy City." We pass a few rooms and Marilyn points out which ones my classes are in. "Most of the sciences are upstairs, since that's where all the labs are. The cafeteria is down this way, to the right, and so is the gym. Back there's the student parking lot. Come on, I'll show you how to open your locker—it's sort of tricky."

I wonder if Marilyn and I will be friends. I doubt it. Not

because of her braces or her wet-dog hair, either. The truth? I've never had a problem landing a guy, but girls tend to be catty and mean, and I've always had trouble making girlfriends. It took nearly two years for Amy Goldstein (who I now consider my BFF) to realize I wasn't trying to get close to her so that I could steal her boyfriend, Trevor (who was gross, by the way); I just wanted to be her friend. There's no doubt in my mind that the girls at East Shore High School will be exactly the same as the previous girls in my life. Maybe worse.

"It must be awful to move senior year," Marilyn says. "If my parents ever did that to me, I would kill them. Lizzie Borden style." She frowns. "No offense."

"It's okay." I don't exactly blame her—moving *does* suck. "I'm trying to be optimistic."

"That's smart," she says. "And East Shore's as decent a school as any, I guess. Do you have a boyfriend?"

Boyfriend. The word zings me. I must make some kind of face, because Marilyn stops in the middle of the hall and blushes. "That was really forward of me. Sorry."

"It's okay," I tell her.

I *did* have a boyfriend.

Ben Harrison. My significant other of the past year (and three months) who told me two days before I left for New

York that we should "take a break" because it would be "really hard to keep in touch . . . you know, especially with the time difference."

I'm pretty sure Ben and I *won't* be getting back together, seeing as how we haven't spoken since I got to Long Island. I count in my head how many text messages I have sent (12) and how many I have received (1).

"No," I respond. "I don't."

Here's the thing: I have this problem with men. Well, boys. I get attached. Really *attached*. I've had my heart broken more times than I can count; each time, I swear off dating until someone new and amazing sweeps me off my feet and makes me forget all the hard parts of falling in love. I am a relationship phoenix: I crash and burn and then I rise and start again. Ben was by far my most serious boyfriend, and I'm exhausted—from crying and trying to figure out what went wrong and how I can possibly fix it. I really thought we had something special, but the fact that he didn't even want to *try* and stay together shows how little he felt in the end. Long distance sucks, but if you love someone, don't you at least want to try?

"Well, there are a few guys at East who'll make your head spin," Marilyn says. "Some of the seniors are *dreamy*."

The last thing I'm interested in is another boyfriend. However, an image of the guy I met at Erica's Sweet Sixteen pops into my head. *Henry.* I wonder what he's doing right now.

"Since you're new, though, just a piece of advice: you'll want to steer clear of the J Squad."

By now, we're at my locker; Marilyn shows me how to enter the combination and continues talking. "They're these three senior girls. They call themselves the J Squad, which is retarded because only two of their names start with J, but whatever. Jyllian, Jessica, and London. They're way snarkilicious, and everyone sort of worships them." She bangs on the metal door and it opens with a squeak. "Here you go."

"The J Squad," I say out loud, trying to picture them. I knew a lot of popular girls back in Chicago who took pleasure in torturing some of the less attractive girls. I was never cool enough to be one of them, but I was also never lame enough to be one of their victims. I've always wondered what it would be like to have a group of friends like that.

"What do they look like?" I ask.

"Oh, you'll know them when you see them," Marilyn says, "but don't be pissed if they don't like you right away.

Or ever. I've heard some *crazy* stories about stuff they do to girls who try to be their friends. They're pretty exclusive."

"Are *you* friends with them?" I ask.

Marilyn snorts. "Definitely not. First, I'm only a sophomore, and second, I don't need to spend time with a bunch of girls who . . . well, you'll see. They can pretty much make or break you, Garrett."

"Don't worry about me," I say. "I'll be fine no matter what. Besides, they sound kind of silly." Then I ask: "So, what period do you have lunch?"

Marilyn tilts her head. "Look, you seem really nice, and I don't know what your last school was like, but at East Shore upperclassmen don't really talk to underclassmen."

"Says who?" I ask.

Marilyn rolls her eyes as if to say *the J Squad.* "Hanging out with me would be social suicide. Trust me." She glances at her watch. "I'm late meeting someone. Good luck."

She scurries away, and I'm left completely alone. I try to remember how to get to my first class, but I can't seem to concentrate. No matter how ridiculous the J Squad sounds, all I can think about is becoming one of them.

BRITNEY SPEARS LYRICS RUNNING THROUGH MY HEAD DURING THE FIRST DAY AT A NEW SCHOOL

"All eyes on me in the center of the ring
just like a circus . . ." —*Circus*

"Sometimes I run, sometimes I hide."
—*Sometimes*

"Hit me baby one more time."
—*. . . Baby One More Time*

School sucks and is mad boring. I try making friends, only no one seems interested in getting to know me. This is both ridiculous and unfair because I'm decent-looking, smart, and not a social d-bag. But for whatever reason, the facts that I'm:

Not from New York
A senior

totally work against me. Perhaps the "new student" intrigue factor might've worked when I was a sophomore or even a junior, but these kids seem resigned to their same old (boring) friends and their same old (boring) lives. There is, apparently, no room for change.

I don't particularly care that my lab partner in physics wants nothing to do with me ("I'm applying early to Cornell. I need to focus") or that when we have to pair off in phys ed, I'm the odd person out and have to do crunches without anyone holding my ankles. (*At least,* I tell myself, *I don't have cankles.*) And it's not that anyone is making fun of me or being outright rude; it's simply that an invisible line exists between belonging and not belonging, a line that seems impossible for me to cross.

I eat lunch alone. Well, not completely alone. I choose a table occupied by two girls and a cluster of empty chairs. The other tables overflow with friends who've known each other for years; the cafeteria, it feels like, is made up of laughter and music coming from the headphones of people's iPods.

"Hi," I say, taking out my lunch (which I brought from home) and placing it in front of me. "I'm Garrett. Is it okay if I sit here?"

They nod.

"So . . . what are your names?"

The girls smile at me. Tell me their names. When I ask how long they've been going to East Shore, they respond with "Since forever," and in the moment it takes me to remove a turkey sandwich from my brown paper bag, they shift their arms and talk quietly in what I think is Korean,

holding a conversation in which I am not invited to partici-
pate. It would, I think, be easier if they'd just tell me to go
away. The silence is what stings.

After lunch, I wish I could just "Relax, Take It Easy"
(Mika, 2007). My binders and books from the morning get
replaced with fresh ones for the afternoon. This is when I
see them.

The J Squad.

Marilyn was right. It's clear who they are from the way
they're dressed (which is not so differently from anyone
else at East Shore but *seems* entirely unique) and the way
they walk: with purpose. They're also gorgeous. Two of
them have long blond hair with waves and curls and body
and bounce, hair that moves as if it's alive. The third has a
cropped black haircut that stays perfectly in place as if by
magic (or some seriously intense hair spray). They have
tight jeans and tight shirts and expensive-looking shoes
that click methodically against the tiled floor in the senior
hallway. Their boobs are semi-to-decently big, their skin is
lightly baked from the summer, and as far as I can tell,
they aren't wearing any makeup. Their bodies seem to be
in perfect proportion. They look like every trio of popular
girls from every teen movie that has ever existed.

I am overwhelmed with jealousy.

They notice me (!) before continuing to their lockers, which are farther down the hall from mine. I think about my table in the cafeteria. About the girls who did not want to include me. What would I be doing if I were back in Chicago? Probably making out with Ben or walking to the nearest Starbucks with Amy.

I turn my attention back to the J Squad. They are laughing and smiling and look incredibly . . . happy. I'm about to approach them when my eye catches on a figure who takes my breath away.

Right there is an incredibly gorgeous guy who is absolutely, for sure, staring at me. He's wearing a pair of snug, faded jeans and a yellow T-shirt that, if T-shirts could speak, would say, "Take me off. I know you want to. No need to be gentle." He is tan and muscled and his hair is messy and slightly gelled. His cheeks are smooth and his eyes are dark. He is angular and sexy and everything about him drives me crazy.

He is also familiar.

He's the guy I met at the Sweet Sixteen. The one who I was immediately attracted to. Who left suddenly with no hint that I'd ever see him again. The one I've been (sort of) thinking about ever since.

He goes to my school.

Henry.

HENRY

INT.–EAST SHORE HIGH SCHOOL, TUESDAY, FIRST DAY OF SCHOOL

I freeze when I see her. What is she doing here? I think back to the party and remember her mentioning that she'd just moved, and it all clicks into place. She now goes to East Shore. I do not know what to feel, so I feel nothing. I just watch.

NIGEL

I can't fit any of my books in this backpack. It's
too small.

DUKE

That's what she said.

NIGEL

What?

DUKE

That's what she said. It's a joke.

NIGEL

I know. It's stupid.

DUKE

Your mom's stupid.

NIGEL

Henry, make him stop.

DUKE

Yo, Enrico. Isn't that the girl you banged last week?

Never in a million years did I imagine I would see this girl again. Garrett. I'd hoped I would, but I have hoped for a lot of things in my life. I know from experience that *hope* does not equal *happening*.

DUKE

You all right, Enrico? Henry? Hello?

ME

I'm fine.

I blink. She's still there. Wearing a black shirt and a dark pair of jeans. She looks gorgeous. The vibe in the hallway changes, as if a button has been pressed and everyone around me stops, waiting to see what I will do. If I act happy to see Garrett, then she means something to me. If I act nonchalant, then she means nothing.

What will I do?

GARRETT

Henry?

I push Duke and Nigel away but I know they are not out of earshot.

ME

I, uh, didn't expect to run into you.

GARRETT

Ditto.

ME

So . . . you go to school here?

Dumb, dumb, dumb. Why else would she be here?

GARRETT

Yeah. Well, it's my first day. But yeah.

ME

Are you liking it?

GARRETT

It's okay. I haven't really made any friends yet.
It's . . . really good to see you, Henry. It's nice to
run into someone I know. Well, someone I sort
of know.

ME

What class do you have next?

GARRETT

Spanish. I don't even know why I'm taking it, really.
It's not like I can say anything useful except <u>Creo</u>
<u>que vomité por allá. Lo siento.</u>

[TRANSLATION: I think I vomited over there. Sorry.]

ME

Looks good on college applications.

GARRETT

I guess. How about you?

ME

I'm off this period.

GARRETT

Too bad we don't have lunch together. (She pouts.
It's adorable.) That would be fun.

Duke and Nigel choose this moment to interrupt.

DUKE

Remember us?

NIGEL

Surprise, surprise.

GARRETT

I do. (She laughs, softly.) Nice to see you
guys again.

DUKE

(checking her out)

It's nice to see <u>you</u> again. Isn't it nice, Nigel?

NIGEL

Sure is. So, what's your name, mystery girl?

GARRETT

Garrett.

DUKE

Do you have a boyfriend, Garrett?

I wait for her answer.

GARRETT

Why, are you offering? (To Duke.) Charlie von
Huseldorf, right? Oil money?

Duke blushes.

GARRETT (cont.)

What are you doing later, Henry?

ME

Oh . . . I dunno. Stuff.

I feel the burn of Duke's and Nigel's eyes on the back of my neck.

GARRETT

(lowering her voice)

Would you maybe want to get a cup of coffee?

Yes, I want to say. But Duke and Nigel think I've already hooked up with her. How would I explain myself? I am Henry Arlington. I do not get with the same girl twice. I do not get coffee. I do not have girlfriends.

ME

Maybe some other time. (The second bell rings and whatever hold has been over the hallway dissolves. People start to move.) See ya.

I walk away and don't look back. I'm scared that if I do, I will see something that will make me change my mind.

I don't dislike being by myself—in fact, I sort of prefer it. Most days, when I get home from school, I sit down at the piano and play, or put my iTunes on shuffle and listen to whatever my computer tells me I should be listening to; or I'll watch random (silly) YouTube videos on my computer. And do my homework. My dad works late; sometimes we'll have dinner together, but mostly I cook myself something simple (chicken, fish, vegetables, pasta) and eat at the kitchen table with my dog, Max, at my feet. I'll go online for a few minutes, take a shower, flick on the TV in my room, and chill out to one of the *hundreds* of DVDs I own. There's not a night in recent history I can remember *not* falling asleep to a movie, whether it's something indie or big-budget or whatever. I will watch anything once. I will watch anything *good* twice. Or more than twice. (This is a secret: I've seen *Shakespeare in Love*, like, twenty times. Seriously. Don't tell anyone.)

Right now I am working my way through all the Scorsese films. I've been going by decade; I started with the seventies—*Mean Streets; Taxi Driver; New York, New York; Alice Doesn't Live Here Anymore; The Last Waltz; American Boy*—and have moved on to the eighties. I'm in the middle of *Raging Bull;* I love that it's in black-and-white, and how Scorsese messes with perspective to get across his point of view. I admire how involved he was in shaping the script. I think he is a brilliant story-teller.

I walk and feed Max every day after school, and today is no different. When I'm done, I finish my calculus problem set—why do teachers give assignments on the first day of school? What's the point?—and go outside to play a little basketball. I debate whether to call Duke and Nigel to come over, but I decide against it. Even though they haven't done anything wrong, I'm a little pissed at them. Or at myself. I can't really tell which.

The three of us came up with the Crasher Code last year so that we *wouldn't* wind up with girlfriends who'd drag us down our last year in high school and make our lives miserable. Because even when it starts out all fun and isn't-this-so-great?, that is what girls do: complicate things. They make requests and place demands and pretty soon you go from carefree to completely stressed. That's the very *last* thing I want for myself. I want my freedom. I want to do whatever I please, whatever makes me happy. So why can't I stop thinking about Garrett?

I toss the ball into my garage and go inside. Upstairs, I pull out the piece of paper with the Crasher Code that Nigel wrote out one night. I don't know why I saved it, exactly, but I look at it every now and then.

THE CRASHER CODE

Rule #1: Never tell a girl your real name

Rule #2: No hos before bros

Rule #3: Never get with the same girl twice

Rule #4: Never spend more than five minutes talking to the same person (unless it's a chick and you're about to seal the deal)

Rule #5: Never contradict another crasher

Rule #6: Do your research

Rule #7: Never wear spandex or anything that can be mistaken for spandex

Rule #8: Wrap it before you tap it

Rule #9: Always compliment the birthday girl, but never bone her

Rule #10: Always be (kind of) polite

Rule #69: Decide on a meeting spot beforehand, and if there's an emergency . . . drop everything and run!

I laugh to myself as I think about some of the ridiculous things I have done with these guys. Stealing the birthday cake at a Sweet Sixteen in Glen Cove and drawing a penis on it in vanilla icing. Pretending to be Danish royalty and dancing with seventy-year-old ladies at a Sweet Sixteen in Little Neck. Toasting the birthday girl (while posing as interns for *Newsday*) at a Sweet Sixteen in Old Bethpage. Dancing, drinking, hooking up, more drinking, more dancing. More hooking up.

Could I give that all up for a girl? Would I have to? Could I have both: independence *and* a girlfriend? I have gone so long without being responsible for anyone's happiness but my own that I don't even know if such a thing is possible. Being happy with someone else. Being *with* someone else. The notion is completely foreign to me, like somewhere far, far away that can only be reached by a boat or a plane or a hot-air balloon.

I wake to the sound of my father coming home; downstairs, Max barks in excited yips. I glance at the clock on my nightstand: 10:49 p.m. Is it too late to call Garrett? I don't even have her number.

DAD

Henry? You up?

ME

(yelling downstairs)

I am now!

I stumble to our kitchen. My father is rummaging through the fridge. Dad works a finance job in Manhattan. Good pay but crappy hours. He's up early and gets back late.

DAD

Oh, there you are. How was school?

ME

Fine.

DAD

First day back, eh?

ME

Yup.

DAD

Hard classes?

ME

Sort of.

DAD

You'll do fine. You always do.

That exchange, I think, pretty much sums up our relationship. We are not buddies and we are not friends. We are father and son, but we keep a safe distance from one another. He cares about me—I know that much—but he was so in love with my mother that when she left, it broke him. We are holding on to each other by threads, he and I, afraid that if we do or say anything too drastic, the threads will unravel completely.

I watch him make a sandwich and open a cold beer. I imagine how this scene would play out in a Scorsese film. Some dramatic underscoring? A shot with the brightness of the refrigerator illuminating the dark kitchen? A close-up of my face? Of his?

He goes to sit in the living room, and I hear him turn on the TV. There is nothing stopping me from joining him, but there is also nothing encouraging me to. This is our routine.

I go back upstairs and get ready for bed. I put on a fresh pair of boxers and a clean T-shirt that says the name of my elementary school on it. I turn on *Raging Bull*. I'm up to the part when DeNiro, who plays Jake LaMotta, a middle-weight boxer, knocks down the door to the bathroom where his wife is hiding, demanding to know whether she had an affair with his brother (played by Joe Pesci). DeNiro is an animal and I love it.

I watch for about twenty minutes and then turn it off. Some people like to see movies from the beginning to the end. No interruptions. I get that, but if I have a choice, I like to watch them in pieces, to savor them, like an expensive steak or a good book.

My father has retreated to his bedroom; I can see the light underneath his door. The rest of the house is dark. I go into the hallway and wait, listening. I do this most nights. Sometimes, I hear nothing. Other times I hear sounds that make me wish I'd never listened in the first place.

Grown men are not supposed to cry. Especially fathers. They are supposed to be protectors; they are supposed to be strong. But my father is not strong. He is weak. On the outside he looks whole, but inside there are pieces missing, chunks of him that my mother scooped away and took with her when she left us. *I'm going, baby. I'm sorry, but I have to go.* One day she was there and the next she was not, and my father, who loved her with everything he had to love her with, slowly began to fade. Thanks to my mother, I have always known there is a difference between loneliness and aloneness. I am alone, but my father is lonely. And if I had to choose one, I would rather be alone.

In my room, I put the Crasher Code back where it belongs. I am an idiot for wasting any time thinking about a girl named Garrett who I barely know. Because there is one solid truth about women, and that is this: they never stay.

GARRETT

It takes three full days before the J Squad asks me to have lunch with them. Part of me thought it would never happen. Overall, I am pleased. Marilyn has basically disappeared, and Erica, whose Sweet Sixteen I attended, hangs out with a bunch of girls who chain-smoke in the student parking lot and seem about as approachable as pit bulls.

I have yet to make a single new friend at East Shore.

Jessica is the one who begins. "We asked you to have lunch with us today because you're new."

The four of us are at a table smack in the middle of the cafeteria. Prime real estate.

"And you're pretty," Jyllian adds. "Well, you're sort of pretty."

"Pretty-ish," says Jessica.

"Thanks?"

"You're welcome," says London. I can't tell for sure, but I think she's in charge. She is the only one without a name starting with *J* or blond hair; the fact that she's different makes her special. "So, what's your deal?"

"What do you mean?"

"Like, what's your story?"

"My story?"

London smiles at me. Her teeth practically sparkle. "If you were writing a book about your life, and you wrote a chapter, like, every day, what would the chapter you wrote *yesterday* be about?"

"Good one," says Jyllian.

"I guess it would be kind of boring," I say. They stare at me with great intensity, waiting for me to continue. Honestly, I think this particular line of questioning is ridiculous (so what does that say about them?), but this is also the first day at East Shore I haven't had to sit by myself—or virtually by myself—at lunch. People are walking past our table and studying me with interest.

Noticing me. I decide to play along. "I'm still unpacking my stuff from the move, so it would mention that. My homework. Eating dinner. Watching TV. You know, the usual."

"Are you dating anyone?" Jyllian asks.

Jessica widens her eyes. "Yeah, are you?"

I am trying to differentiate between Jyllian and Jessica. It's not easy.

Am I dating anyone? Yes. No. Well . . . no. I did, though. Ben. And what about Henry? I haven't spoken to him since I asked him to have coffee and he blew me off.

I take too long formulating a response; the girls look bored.

"Garrett?"

"No," I say. "Not at the moment." I can't tell if this is the right answer. Was I supposed to say yes so that I didn't seem like a loser? Or is it better to be single—"Miss Independent" (Ne-Yo, 2008)? All I know is that for the first time in a long time, I am completely alone. No boyfriends. No friends (family excluded). Just me.

Jyllian coughs and says, "If I know two things, one of those things is karate. The other is boys. And Garrett, you have boy drama. I can tell just by *looking* at you. I see sadness in your eyes. Spill."

"You don't know karate," Jessica says.

"Oh yeah?" Jyllian raises a hand in the air. "Tell me that after I karate-chop your head off."

"Girls," London says. "Let Garrett speak." She leans forward. "Who dumped you?"

"Is it that obvious?" I ask.

They nod.

"This guy, Ben," I say. "We dated for a while back in Chicago, but I haven't heard from him since I got here. It really . . . sucks."

Sucks doesn't sum it up, but I barely know these girls. I don't need to reveal my life story within ten minutes of meeting them, do I?

Jyllian dabs her eyes with a napkin. "That. Is. Tragic," she says. "Actually, it's *rusty*." She elaborates: "Rusty is when something is so tragic you can't even use *tragic* to describe it." She blinks. "Say it whenever you want. Pay that shit forward."

"Uh, okay," I reply.

"Were you in love?" London asks me, bringing the conversation back to reality.

It's a good question. I liked Ben. He made me laugh. We enjoyed the same movies and listened to (basically) the same music. He was handsome and I had fun hooking up with him. I think he felt the same way about me. But is that *love*? Isn't love something . . . more?

"Yes," I say, because it sounds more dramatic than *I don't know* or *Could you be more specific?* And even if it wasn't love, it still hurts that we're not together, to know he doesn't want me anymore. I do miss him.

London pats my hand. "It's a good thing we found you when we did. We've been watching you, you know."

"You have?"

"I don't know what the girls were like at your last school, or if you had, like, a lot of friends"—London glances at my shoes, and I wonder if she can tell how many friends I had by the kind of shoes I wear—"but at East Shore we're, like, way important."

I'm not sure what the proper response is, so I say, "You guys seem really sweet."

They laugh. "We're definitely not sweet," says Jessica. "But we take care of each other. We've all been through what you're going through with Ben."

"Which is exactly why we *don't* date high school guys," London says. "Ever. It's a rule."

This explains why I haven't seen anyone of the male persuasion attached to their (slim) hips. "A rule?"

"It's like this, Garrett: high school guys are *boys.* They are totally selfish and immature. They will break your heart into a million pieces and then pick up all of the pieces and cut you with them. College guys, on the other hand"—London widens her eyes—"are *men*. You know?"

I don't know. I've never dated anyone in college, nor do I have the desire to. "Well, it's really cool of you to invite me to have lunch with you."

"We know," says London, twisting open a bottle of water. I'm too self-conscious to eat my sandwich in front of these girls; instead, I try convincing myself I'm *not* hungry. It works, but barely.

"Don't get used to it," Jessica says.

Oh.

"That's not a threat or anything," London says calmly. "Well, okay, it is, but it's not a *physical* threat."

"Yeah, we're not going to, like, break your kneecaps with a baseball bat or anything!" Jyllian says, laughing a crazy hyena kind of laugh.

"Should I be scared?" I ask.

London raises her eyebrows. "Of us?"

"Um, yeah."

"Here's the deal, Garrett," Jessica says. "We've been friends since seventh grade."

"We used to be friends with another girl named Jennifer," says Jyllian, "but . . . we're not anymore."

"I'm sorry," I say, because I'm uncomfortable.

"Don't be," says London, waving her hand dismissively. "She was mad trashy. Anyway, you seem like you'd fit in well with us. Public school can be rough, especially because we're going to graduate this year. Hanging out with us would do *wonders* for your social life, which, we're guessing, is pretty nonexistent."

Truthfully, these girls don't seem like the kind of people I would be friends with if I had my choice. I think about my best friend back in Chicago, Amy, who would literally have convulsions if she ever saw me with girls who had a group nickname. But Amy isn't here now. I am. And so far, the J Squad are the only ones who seem remotely interested in having me around.

Now, I'm not totally naïve—I've seen enough movies to know that:

High School + Pretty Girls = Bad News

The popular clique never makes for the best friends. That's just not how it works. But let's face it: I moved halfway across the country for senior year. What's the likelihood I'll make any *real* friends?

"That sounds great," I say.

London smirks. "Oh, sweetie. It's not *that* easy."

"What do you mean?"

"You can't just become one of us right away," Jyllian scoffs. "I mean, that's not how friendship works."

"It's not?"

"*It's not,*" Jessica says knowingly. "You have to earn it. For now, you can be our friend on a trial basis."

"What that means," London says, "is that you can hang out with us before, during, and after school, and on the weekends until the end of October."

"What happens at the end of October?" I ask.

"Destiny Monroe's Sweet Sixteen," Jyllian says. "It's being filmed for an episode of MTV's *My Super Sweet Sixteen* and it's going to be *epic.* Like, so lavish."

"*Lavish,*" Jyllian says, "is the opposite of rusty. Just FYI."

"How do I fit in?" I ask.

"You don't," London says. "*Yet.* Do you see that guy?" She points into the courtyard where Henry and his friends are throwing a tennis ball against one of the brick walls.

"Yeah."

"His name is Henry Arlington," Jessica says. "He's by far the sexiest guy at East Shore—"

"On all of Long Island," Jyllian interjects. "And Long Island is, like . . . *long.* It looks like a fish."

"Thanks for that brilliant insight," London says. "Anyway, Henry is *totally* edible but a major prick. He thinks he's better than everyone. Even us."

I'm about to ask if any of them have dated him, but I hold back. "Why are you telling me this?"

"If you can get Henry to publicly acknowledge you as his girlfriend and take you, as his date, to Destiny Monroe's Sweet Sixteen," London say, "you can officially join the J Squad."

"And if I don't?"

"You can't hang out with us anymore, and we'll make your life at East Shore a living hell. And Garrett? We can do that."

She is so serious it makes me want to laugh. (I don't, though.) Do they know about Henry and me? Not that anything has ever happened between us. He won't even look at me.

"Once you're at the party," London says, "you have to dump him on camera in front of *everyone*. It'll prove to us that you're above dating high school boys *and* it will be the ultimate payback."

"Payback for what?" I ask.

Jyllian and Jessica exchange glances. London ignores them and continues: "Henry is a heartbreaker. He's hurt more girls than you can imagine. He deserves to know what that feels like for once."

"No offense," I say, "but that's assuming I could even get him to date me, let alone like me enough so he would actually be upset when I dump him."

London appears unfazed. "Right."

I gulp. What London is proposing is actually, well, cruel. And while Henry *did* blow me off for coffee, he didn't ruin my life. I don't know what he's done to deserve such malice.

"I'm not sure I can do that," I say. "Henry seems . . . nice. Nice enough, at least. No offense."

Jessica fakes gagging. "He's about as nice as getting a huge pimple on your forehead right before you're competing in a Teen Miss Long Island Sound pageant and losing out to a girl from Great Neck with tacky extensions and inappropriate tan lines." She lets out a tiny burp. "Or whatever."

"I guess it's true, then," Jyllian says, turning to London.

"I guess," London agrees.

"What's true?" I ask.

"We heard that you and Henry hooked up at a party before school started." London grabs her purse, as if she's about to leave. "What you *don't* know is that he never hooks up with the same girl twice. So if you think you're gonna be, like, *an item* or something . . . I'd seriously reconsider."

I'm stunned. "You heard what?"

"You mean you *didn't* hook up with him?" Jyllian asks.

"Absolutely not," I tell them, omitting the fact that I probably would have if he hadn't left the party so quickly. "Who did you hear that from?"

London rests her purse on the table. "Everyone's talking about it. But I heard it from Duke. And there's only one person *he* could have heard it from."

I don't want to believe that Henry lied to his friends about us getting together. "Why would he lie about that?"

Jessica puts her arm around me. "Maybe he wants people to think you're a slut."

I cringe. This happened to me once before, when I was a freshman at my old school. This senior named Mark and I were talking at a house party, and we hit it off. The next day, however, everyone at Mercer thought we'd had sex. Turns out he was a total asshole and spread rumors about me. It took months until people stopped thinking I was easy. To this day, I still despise him. I can't believe Henry falls in the same ranks. He seemed . . . different.

"This is what Henry does," London says, pushing Jessica out of the way, placing her hand on my shoulder. "He deserves to be punished."

I reconsider the J Squad's offer. The positives of this arrangement:

- Instant popularity
- A secure group of friends—at least for the year
- Getting back at Henry for giving me a reputation at East Shore before I had time to establish one myself

The negatives:

- Spending time with Henry (He lied to people about us hooking up *and* had the nerve to blow me off earlier!)
- Spending time with the J Squad (They seem kinda fake and slightly insane.)
- Compromising my morals (Do I even *have* morals?)

I realize that trying to get Henry to be my boyfriend just so I can hang out with the J Squad and eventually dump him is wrong. It's "Mean" (John Mellencamp, 2008). But Henry hasn't exactly been nice to me, and it's not like I want to actually date him. I don't want a boyfriend. I want *friends*. And isn't this what these girls are offering? Friendship? Even if it's completely artificial? Does that mean it can't potentially grow into something . . . more?

The bell rings; I cannot believe forty-five minutes have passed so quickly.

"You have the weekend to think about it," says London. "If you're not interested, we'll leave you alone. No harm done. If you *are* interested, well"—she slips me a napkin with her phone number written on it—"that's another story. Have a nice day, Garrett."

I watch the J Squad leave, and I'm not the only one. The entire cafeteria observes their exit. I close my eyes and picture myself with them. I am surprised at how easily the image comes.

Then I open my eyes and they are gone. Everyone's attention is back to his or her respective table. No one is watching me.

At home, my mother is dancing around the kitchen table; freshly brewed coffee and chocolate-covered graham crackers are waiting for me.

"What's all this for?"

"Oh, just something I cooked up," she says, swiveling her hips and jingling her bracelets in the air.

"You didn't *cook* anything. The coffee is from Dunkin' Donuts and the graham crackers are from . . . I don't know. The supermarket."

"You're always so concerned with details, Garrett," Mom says, continuing to shimmy. "That's why you can never keep a boyfriend. Well, that and you're a total pushover."

"Mom!"

"It's true," she says, kissing my forehead.

"You don't have to be mean about it," I say. "And I am *not* a pushover."

"If you say so, sweetie."

My mother, by the way, is the closest thing I have to a best friend besides Amy. We have a very casual relationship despite her being a total kook. "Name one time I was a pushover."

"Just one? Fine. Andrew Carrington."

I shoot her a dirty look. Andrew Carrington was my first high school *romance*. We dated for six months toward the end of ninth grade (he was a senior), during which he introduced me to many "bad" things that I did simply because he asked me to.

Andrew, on beer: "It's good for you."

Andrew, on pot: "It's good for you."

Andrew, on letting him feel me up: "I think one of your boobs is bigger than the other. I should probably check to make sure."

I told my mom everything we did partly because I felt guilty and partly because I had no one else to tell.

"Low blow. I was fifteen."

"That's only one example, honey. I love you, but when it comes to boys you sort of lose control."

MADONNA LYRICS RUNNING THROUGH MY HEAD WHEN I THINK ABOUT SOME OF MY PREVIOUS RELATIONSHIPS

"Waiting for your call baby night and day, I'm fed up, I'm tired of waiting on you." —*Hung Up*

"Papa don't preach, I'm in trouble deep."
—*Papa Don't Preach*

~~**"Like a virgin, touched for the very first time"**~~
~~**—*Like a Virgin***~~

I am slightly aggravated only because she's right. "It's a good thing I'm done with boys, then."

My mother feigns shock. "Since when?"

"Since today," I tell her, picturing Henry and then Ben. "I'm through with them. *Forever.*"

"Forever?"

I think about it. "Well, until college."

That gets a laugh out of her. "Okay, Garrett. Let's see how long that lasts, hmm?"

Upstairs, I take out my guitar and sit on the edge of my bed. I'm no great musician, but I love the feel of my fingers on the strings, the sound of changing chords. If I had a killer voice or a thousand melodies in my head, I'd want to be a singer-songwriter, like Joni Mitchell or Ani DiFranco or Tift Merritt. I have written some lyrics, but they're more melodramatic than meaningful.

I love all kinds of music, really. Old-fashioned rock and roll, country, bluegrass, and—of course—Top 40 pop. As long as I can hum along and forget my troubles for a little while, I'm good. My favorite songs are love songs. Happy ones for when I'm happy, sad ones for when I'm sad. Listening to a song where the singer has gone through the same stuff I'm going through makes me feel like someone, somewhere, understands me—and if other people have experienced heartbreak, surely mine can't be *that* bad.

When you've been dumped as many times as I have, the initial sting tends to dissipate quickly. I used to cry for weeks and weeks over boys—over not being wanted anymore, over what we could have been but never had the chance to be. But that slowly faded, until a relationship would end and I'd move forward, only to be smacked with grief when I least expected it, the kind of pain that attacks you from behind and doesn't let go.

This makes me sound like some kind of relationship whore. I'm not—not really. I've only had five real boyfriends.

(Ex-) Boyfriend #1: Johnny Rosenfeld
Year we dated: Eighth grade
Looks: Sort of cute; not pimply
Really into: The Dave Matthews Band
First thing he ever said to me: "You're so funny."
Last thing he ever said to me: "You cry a lot."

(Ex-) Boyfriend #2: Andrew Carrington
Year we dated: Ninth grade
Looks: Sexxxy
Really into: Himself
First thing he ever said to me: "You're, like, really hot."
Last thing he ever said to me: "Can you get your own ride home?"

(Ex-) Boyfriend #3: Dan Girwager

Year we dated: Tenth grade

Looks: Hot nerd

Really into: Getting good grades

First thing he ever said to me: "You like F. Scott Fitzgerald too?"

Last thing he ever said to me: "You're just really . . . *different* than I am. And not in a good way."

(Ex-) Boyfriend #4: Michael Brown

Year we dated: Tenth grade (second half)

Looks: B-list movie star–ish

Really into: His band

First thing he ever said to me: "I've never met anyone like you, Garrett."

Last thing he ever said to me: "Please stop calling my house."

(Ex-) Boyfriend #5: Ben Harrison

Year we dated: Eleventh grade plus the summer

Looks: Boy next door

Really into: Basketball

First thing he ever said to me: "Is anyone sitting here?"

Last thing he ever said to me: ?

I don't know the last thing Ben will ever say to me. I think about how many hours I've spent crying over him. I can't go through that again with another guy. Then I think about Henry lying to his friends about us hooking up, and what Mark did to me years ago. I realize the J Squad is right: high school guys really *are* boys. How could Henry start that rumor with no regard for my feelings? And even if he didn't start it—if Nigel or Duke did—he should have been mature enough to reveal the truth. Instead, he'd rather let people think I'm another tally on his scoreboard.

Well, screw that. The J Squad may be a little over the top, but they definitely have the right idea. Someone like Henry *does* need to know what it feels like to be hurt. And if anyone's an expert on getting dumped, it's me—why *shouldn't* I be the one to teach him a lesson?

Seducing Henry will be a challenge, sure, but I can do it. There's no way I'll develop real feelings for a guy I know is a player from the start. Even though it will *seem* to the average East Shore outsider like we're dating, it'll all be a game—a game in which *I* make the rules. If my heart isn't on the line, there's no way I can possibly get hurt. And if I can't get hurt, what's there to lose? Plus, having the J Squad in my life would certainly help me avoid falling for anyone else. Even my mother doesn't think I can go without a (real) boyfriend. It's time, I decide, to prove her wrong. To prove them all wrong. To make boys like Henry and Ben and Mark and [insert practically every high school guy in existence] realize what it feels like to be dumped, to be crushed, to be broken.

And to prove to myself that I can be strong, and happy, without being in a relationship.

I put down my guitar, pick up my cell, and punch in some numbers I've already memorized. "London? It's Garrett Lennox. Count me in."

HENRY

INT.—MY CAR, SATURDAY NIGHT

Duke, Nigel, and me pull into the parking lot of a Hilton hotel. A girl named Rosie Black is having her Sweet Sixteen tonight. Duke heard about the party from his friend Brian, who goes to high school with Rosie in Great Neck and hooked up with her once, but it ended badly. (Somehow Brian woke up in her driveway wearing lipstick, gym shorts, and a shirt that read *Who's Your Daddy?*)

I park and we get out of the car.

ME

Everyone has the story down, right?

DUKE

Yes, Mom.

ME

I'm not your mother.

DUKE

That's what she said. You know, when I was
doing her.

NIGEL

I hate those jokes. I really do.

We begin our trek into the Hilton. We don't have an invitation, but that's never stopped us before. We're wearing suits and we're young—it's surprisingly easy.

Tonight, Duke and I are pretending to be fraternal conjoined twins who were only recently separated. (This is not actually possible.) Nigel will be a foreign exchange student from Canada who is staying with us. (We chose Canada because, well, it's so ridiculous!)

We enter the hotel and immediately turn left; we've been here before. It's a pretty hoppin' venue for a Sweet Sixteen because there's a themed fifties diner on the bottom floor. It looks like a (slightly) classier Johnny Rockets. I know we're in the right place because I hear music.

The room is packed—there are at least two hundred people here, which means we'll go basically unnoticed. On first glance, there are tons of hot girls. Score.

Duke gets mixed up in the crowd within seconds. Most of the kids here are from Great Neck, which means they're very rich and/or Persian.

NIGEL

I'm thirsty. Grab me a Coke?

ME

Sure. (I locate an empty booth with a balloon centerpiece and shove him inside.) Be right back.

I walk up to the bar and ask for a Coke *and* a gin and tonic. The bartender gives me the Coke (in an actual glass bottle) but not the G + T. Ah, well. Can't blame a guy for trying.

I sit down next to Nigel and hand him the bottle. He looks at it quizzically.

NIGEL

This feels so . . . elegant.

ME

Only the best for you, man. Only the best.

I turn my attention to the dance floor. Most of the girls are wearing T-shirts that say *Melissa's Sweet 16* over their dresses, which I think is a travesty, and white socks over their tights instead of shoes. I don't fault them for that. I can't imagine getting my groove on in a pair of high heels. That shit must hurt.

I bop my head along to the music and feel happy. I'd like to be dancing, sure, but I don't mind just being surrounded by a bunch of random people who don't expect anything from me. I think for a moment about Garrett, because we met at a party not all that different from this one, but only for a moment. I'm here to have fun. And I can *certainly* have fun with*out* Garrett.

My eyes move to a really pretty girl who's sitting with a bunch of other, less pretty girls at one of the booths diagonal to mine; she has long red hair and is wearing a dress with no straps and her boobs look *sweet*. I glance over at Nigel, who is touching the Coke bottle lightly with his index finger.

ME

Can I leave you alone for a second?

NIGEL

Yeah, no worries. Do yo thang.

ME

I won't be long. And you probably shouldn't say 'yo' and 'thang' in the same sentence.

NIGEL

Point taken.

I find a spot where it's a little less noisy. I look back at the girl; she's already left her table and is walking in my direction. One for Arlington.

ME

Hey.

HER

Hey. Do I know you?

ME

Do you want to?

HER

(laughing)

Yes?

ME

That's a good start. I'm Angel.

HER

That's an . . . interesting name. Like

the guy from <u>Buffy</u>?

ME

No.

HER

From the musical <u>Rent</u>?

ME

No.

HER

Where do you go to school? Great Neck South?

ME

I'm homeschooled.

HER

Yeah? For any particular reason?

ME

My brother and I were conjoined twins, but, uh, now

we're not.

HER

That's not . . . really a reason.

ME

It's not?

HER

How do you know Melissa?

ME

Family friends.

HER

(leaning in close)

I'm her cousin. <u>Older</u> cousin. I'm a junior at Penn
State. I have the key to one of the hotel rooms
upstairs. (She cocks her head.) Care to join me?

No girl has ever been so frank with me before. I check in
on Nigel, who's still fascinated by the Coke bottle. He'll be
fine. Duke is nowhere to be seen.

ME

Lead the way.

As soon as we close the door to her room, I yank off my
suit jacket, pull off my tie, and drop my pants.

HER

Whoa, there, cowboy. Slow down.

ME

Is something wrong?

HER

We just met.

ME

I thought you invited me up here to . . . you know.

She slips her shoes off and waltzes over to the minibar.

HER

I <u>invited</u> you up here to get to know you better.
It was so loud down there. (She pauses.)
Want a drink?

I'm kind of embarrassed. I don't want to make the scene more awkward than it already is, so I button my pants, toss my suit jacket and tie on the bed, and nod my head.

HER (cont.)

There aren't any mixers, so we'll just
have to go for it.

She grabs two tiny bottles and motions to a sliding glass door that leads to a balcony. We go outside; it's dark, and there's not much of a view, but the air is light and cool. I sit down on one of the chairs.

HER

So what's your real name?

ME

Huh?

HER

You don't look like an Angel.

ME

Oh. Um, well . . . it's Henry.

HER

I'm Lila.

She passes me one of the bottles, but I have to drive later, so I refuse. She shrugs and drinks it herself, grimacing as it goes down. We both laugh. Her laugh is nice—not like Garrett's, which is heartier, and more musical—but nice nonetheless.

LILA

How do you really know my cousin?

ME

Family friends. I told you.

LILA

Uh-huh, sure. (She looks at me.) You're cute.
Young, but cute.

ME

I'm not that young.

LILA

How old are you?

ME

Eighteen. Well, seventeen. But I'll be eighteen soon.

LILA

How soon?

ME

A coupla months.

LILA

Trust me, kid. You're young.

ME

You're what, twenty? Not exactly ancient.

LILA

I don't mean young year-wise. Just life-wise. (She
wipes a few strands of hair away from her eyes.)
College changes you. The whole world opens up.
You'll see.

ME

I can't wait to go. I want to get the hell out of here.

LILA

Long Island?

I nod.

LILA (cont.)

It's not that bad. But I hear you. Don't rush your
senior year away, though. That's time you'll never
get back.

We're pretty high up. In the distance I can see cars driving along the highway. Below us is an outside restaurant
where people are having dinner. I don't have much else to
say, really. Lila seems nice, but there's no real spark. I
think about some of the girls I've hooked up with recently.
Everything happens so quickly it's hard to say if there's

ever a real connection. I'm not sure I would know a spark if it set me on fire. Then I think about Garrett and I know that's not true. I realized the moment I saw her there was a spark. That she sparkled.

It's getting kind of chilly. I notice Lila shiver and move my chair closer. I touch her shoulder. She has goose bumps.

ME

Here.

I run my fingers up and down her arms, lightly.

LILA

That feels good. It tingles.

I lean forward and kiss her shoulder. Then her neck. She turns her head and pecks me on the lips.

LILA (cont.)

You're sweet, Henry. You're gonna make someone
a great boyfriend someday.

I want to laugh. If only she knew how messed up I am, she'd never say anything like that. Me? A great boyfriend? I don't think so.

ME

You wanna head back to the party?

LILA

That's probably a good idea. I'm sure my parents
are looking for me, wanting to take pictures
or something.

She goes back into the room. I'm about to slide the balcony door shut when I stop and take a second to stare into the night and just breathe. I feel as though I have as many questions as there are stars.

We're in my car, driving home. It's almost one in the morning. I don't have a curfew, but Nigel does. He's in the backseat, sleeping, still holding on to the (now empty) Coke bottle.

DUKE

So, did you have fun? I saw you go upstairs with
that cute redhead.

ME

You did?

                    DUKE
               (elbowing me)
                  Get any?

                     ME
              Uh, you could say that.

                    DUKE
      Nice, dude. <u>Nice.</u> One of these days, you've gotta
                 tell me your secret.

                     ME
              Sure. One of these days.

We drive the rest of the way home listening to Bruce
Springsteen's *Magic* album. I can't help but realize I *don't*
love Sweet Sixteens—not like I used to. Have I outgrown
crashing parties? No, that's ridiculous. But what, then, has
changed?

The next morning, I wake up around noon and cook myself some eggs. I shoot a couple of hoops outside, then
check my e-mail. Soon, it's almost two p.m. I shower,
shave, and leave so I can grab a cup of coffee and get to
work by three.

I've worked at the Huntington Cinemas since I was six-teen. It's a bit out of the way from where I live (about a twenty-five-minute drive), but it's the best independent movie house on Long Island. Hands down. My boss, Roger, pretty much lets me do whatever I want, and I get to see all the films for free. I also help pick which films to show, which is awesome, because Roger basically knows nothing about movies. (I'm not sure what he actually *is* knowl-edgeable about, but that's another story.)

I love my job. I love that all I have to do is scan tickets or help people choose what movie they want to see or take their money and give them change or direct them to which theater they'll be sitting in. Sometimes shit hits the fan (or overflows the toilet), and I do have to clean the theaters—which kind of blows—but mostly it's pretty calm. Unlike at school, where everyone wants a piece of me, the other employees mostly let me be. They get that I'm not much of a talker.

The Huntington Cinemas is my refuge, my home away from home, where I go to leave the world behind. Which is why I'm shocked when I see *her* standing in the middle of the lobby.

Garrett.

Turning up for the second time without any warning.

6

GARRETT

Henry looks surprised to see me.

Surprised doesn't really capture it, though. More like *horrified.* I decide to take his reaction as a compliment.

I'm wearing a nice pair of jeans and a curve-enhancing sweater. I'm unsure what the qualifications for working in a movie theater are (Not stealing candy? Being able to count without using your fingers?), but I'm kind of nervous. I don't want to apply for a job here and get *rejected.* How embarrassing.

"Garrett? What are you doing here?"

He's wearing the same uniform as the other employees, but somehow Henry Arlington makes yellow, black, and a name tag look good.

"Nice to see you too."

"I mean, hey." He tugs on the collar of his shirt. "What's up?"

"Not much. Just here to apply for a job."

"You want to work here? Why?"

"Why not?" I ask.

"It's not exactly glamorous," he says, motioning to the concession area, where a girl with red hair (and an equally red face) is scooping greasy-looking popcorn into a paper bag and coughing. The lobby of the cinema has an old-school Hollywood vibe (plush carpet, white and gold wallpaper, flowing curtains over the windows), but there's something a little run-down about the décor.

Smile. Wink. "You think I'm glamorous?"

"That's not what I meant," Henry says. "I mean . . . you know what I mean. Does the J Squad know you're here?"

I'm tempted to say: *They're the ones who gave me directions and told me what hours you worked.* I don't, though.

("Whatever you do," London instructed me, "do *not* let him think you're applying for a job because of him. And *don't* let on that you know he told people you hooked up, otherwise he'll get suspicious. Just be cool."

"And don't say anything stupid," Jyllian added. "Or slutty.")

I try my best to follow their advice. "No," I say. "Why?"

"You guys seem to do everything together, that's all. I'm surprised they untied your leash for the night."

"There's no leash, Henry. They're my *friends*. That's what you do with friends: spend time together. Besides, we're still getting to know each other, which takes effort."

"I never pinned you as one to follow the masses." He looks at me as though he wants to say something more. I want to say, *You know absolutely nothing about me.* Just then, however, a stocky man approaches us and raises his eyebrows.

"No fraternizing on the job, Arlington," the man says. He has a goatee that seems to be painted on, and his eyes have the glassy sheen of a drug addict or someone with glass eyes. "You know the rules. This isn't a *house party*, or whatever you kids do on the weekends. Don't chat with your lady friend during work hours."

"I'm not," Henry starts to say, "this is—"

"Garrett Lennox," I say, extending my hand. Generally, I'm not into handshakes with random people (all the germs!), but if this guy is Henry's boss—and I assume that he is—then I need to start kissing ass. Or at least being friendly. "I'm not his lady friend. But it's very nice to meet you."

"Huh" is all the man says, scratching his head and giving me a confused look.

"I'm interested in a job," I say, motioning to the lobby.

No response.

"Here."

Still no response.

"At this particular cinema," I say.

"Yeah, yeah, I hear ya." The man frowns. Henry is stifling a laugh. "What are your qualifications?"

"What do you mean?"

"Have you ever worked at a *cinema* before?"

"Well, no."

He narrows his eyes. "Have you ever *worked* before?"

I wonder if he'd count a three-day stint as a Baby Gap salesperson, only I don't mention it because I'm afraid he'll ask why I left, to which I will have to respond that I was fired for hooking up with Ben in one of the dressing rooms during my break.

"Sure," I tell him. "I'd really love to work here. I just moved to Long Island over the summer, and I've heard this place shows great films. I'm a huge movie aficionado."

This is not exactly true. I do know a bit about movies, but not because I'm particularly interested in them. Ex-boyfriend #3, Dan, was very artsy; he used to make me watch foreign films nearly every weekend (with subtitles, of course—he wasn't a monster). It was one of the reasons we eventually broke up. "I like my movies like I like my reality TV shows," I told him. "Trashy. And in English."

Also, and more importantly, my father is a film professor. I've grown up around classic movies and know them as well as I know myself. (Some might argue that's not much, but I would tell those individuals to Suck It.)

The man introduces himself as Roger. I notice that one of his front teeth is gold, and I immediately take a liking to him. "We could use more people around here like you, Gracie," he tells me.

"It's Garrett."

"That's what I said. What kind of hours are you looking for?"

I remember that I'm holding a copy of Henry's schedule, and I give it to him. "These are the hours I'm free."

He nods. "We have a basic training program: any newbie has to shadow one of our current employees for the first few weeks. That person will provide all the details about what's expected of you, blah blah blah. It's not a hard job. I think you'll catch on quickly."

"Thank you," I say.

He looks around; the only employees in sight are Henry,

coughing popcorn girl, and a guy with a busted face who's as skinny as a pencil (if a pencil could be a person). I *must* get paired with Henry. Otherwise, my entire plan is a failure.

I decide on something simple yet effective: "Did you know that Henry and I go to school together?"

Henry glares at me, but Roger doesn't seem to notice. "Arlington," he says, "mind showing Greta here the ropes?"

"Garrett," I repeat. *That was too easy.*

"I don't know," Henry says cautiously, no doubt trying to figure out what my true intentions are.

"What do you mean, 'I don't know'?"

Henry shrugs.

Roger points a stubby finger at him. "Just for that, you *are* going to be in charge of Grizabella over here, and you *will* make sure she doesn't mess up. And if she does"—he shakes his finger—"it's on *you*. Capisce?"

"Yes, sir," Henry says. His expression would make you think he'd been asked to clean someone's puke off the floor. What is it about me that absolutely repels him?

Roger pats me on the shoulder. He reminds me of my (slightly taller) Crazy Uncle Dom, who I actively avoid at family functions. "I'm gonna get your paperwork started, Garrie. You're gonna *love* it here. Just love it."

Roger waddles away and I can't help it—I start laughing. A smile begins to inch across Henry's face, but he manages to stop it.

"So I guess it's just you and me, huh?" I ask.

"I guess."

I think back to the first night I met Henry, and how vibrant he was—how full of life. I was attracted to him immediately. There was something about him, something . . . special. I shake my head, as if the memories will simply fall onto the floor so they can be swept away. *Remember why you're here,* I tell myself. *To win Henry over so you can get even with for him spreading rumors about you and to impress the J Squad. To prove to yourself that you don't need an actual boyfriend to be happy. That's it.*

We're silent until Henry goes, "So why are you really here, Garrett? You don't seem like the type of girl who wants to spend her free time in a dingy movie theater, and you certainly can't be here for the money." He tilts his head. "Are you here because of me? Is that it?"

I feel my jaw unhinge. True, I am kinda stalking him, but that he *assumes* I am really bothers me.

"You think really highly of yourself, don't you? Let me tell you something, *Henry.* I'm here because I love independent cinema and figured it'd be a good way to spend some of my free time. I kind of hoped I would meet some other people who have a passion for movies too, but you're clearly *not* one of those people, so why don't we just save ourselves the trouble and I'll go ask Roger if I can shadow someone else."

I'm here because I love independent cinema? Where did that come from? I'm surprised by how angry I was able to get, especially since everything I just told Henry—well, not everything, but most of it—is a lie. I *am* here because of him. Only he can't *know* that. I have to play Hard To Get.

Henry reacts as if I'd just slapped him. "I have a passion for movies."

"Whatever," I say, although secretly I am thrilled. My little monologue definitely got to him.

"Graciela," a voice calls out. I turn to see Roger coming toward me with a fistful of papers and a black dress shirt with yellow accents on the shoulders. "Here you go." He hands me the shirt and all the papers. "Bring these back filled out, okay? Meanwhile, I'll e-mail you with next week's schedule. Sound good?"

"Yes," I say.

"Sound good to you, Arlington?" Roger asks.

I glance at Henry, waiting for him to interject and say he doesn't want to work with me. It's now or never.

Henry claps his hands together. "Yup, everything's great. I'm just getting *Garrett* here up to speed."

"Don't have *too* much fun," Roger mutters, waddling back into his office. "Kids."

Once he's gone, I look at Henry and wonder what he's thinking. "Better go get changed," he tells me. "We've got work to do."

"So what was it like?" Jessica asks me the next day in the cafeteria, sifting through the contents of her unnecessarily large purse and pulling out a pair of chopsticks.

"Why do you have those?" I ask.

"You never know when you might need them."

It's funny how in high school (and, I suspect, in the real world), being friends with the right people really does matter. Already this morning, four random girls have complimented me on my jeans, and one guy in my AP Lit class told me I looked like Natalie Portman. (At which I blushed and said, "Oh, stop," but really I was flattered.) That definitely would *not* have happened if I weren't the newest (on a trial basis) member of the most popular clique at East Shore.

"Tell us *everything*," Jyllian insists, dipping her finger into a fat-free Jell-O pudding cup and licking it.

There's honestly not much to tell. Henry showed me around the movie theater and explained how to use the register, how to scan the tickets, and where to direct patrons if they needed to use a bathroom. Our conversation was . . . cordial. I could tell he was holding back, not being entirely himself. Henry is going to be tougher to crack than I originally anticipated, but I can do it. I can *definitely* do it.

"Tell us about *Henry*," Jessica says. Today she's wearing her hair in a long braid down her back, which sounds milkmaid-ish, but it's actually a good look for her. She takes a jar of peanut butter, a slice of bread, and a knife out of her bag and starts to make a sandwich—no one even flinches at how odd this is.

What do I say? I don't want to lie and say that Henry and I hit it off, but I also don't want them to think I won't be able to seal the deal.

I go with: "He was really surprised to see me there."

"Of course he was," London says. "What else?"

I tell them I'll be shadowing him for the next few weeks. They seem very, very pleased and genuinely "Interested" (India.Arie, 2002) in what I have to say.

"You didn't mention hearing about the rumor, did you?"

"No."

"Good," London says, sounding relieved. "That means you still have the upper hand."

I don't get why it's so important to keep my knowledge of the rumor a secret. My instinct is to be completely transparent and curse him out. "Wouldn't he assume I know, though?"

London shakes her head. "Not necessarily. Henry lives in his own world. He thinks he's, like, some kind of *artist* or something. But he's not fooling me."

I want to ask how well London and Henry know each other, but the subject seems kind of taboo; I decide to wait for the right moment to bring it up—whenever that'll be.

"Who wants to go for iced coffees after school?" Jessica asks, chewing on the end of her braid. "I'm parched. And then mani/pedis?"

London and Jyllian both say, "Absolutely." They look at me. "You're coming, right?"

I smile back, not because I want an iced coffee or to get my nails done, but because I have girlfriends inviting me to hang out with them. It feels almost too good to be true.

HENRY

INT.–HUNTINGTON CINEMAS BREAK ROOM,
SUNDAY

It's been a full week since Garrett landed a job at my
movie theater, and I'm still not used to having my private
space invaded. Huntington Cinemas has been my hide-
away since I was sixteen. I feel violated. Annoyed.
Also intrigued.

One of the guys I work with, Tony Macharetti, pats me on the shoulder as I stuff my bag in my locker and put on my uniform.

TONY

Yo, Arlington. Good weekend so far?

ME

Sure. You?

TONY

My dog is sick. My ma fed him turkey meatballs and
now he won't stop barfing. It's gross.

Tony is a senior at West Shore, our rival high school. Not that I play into the rivalry.

TONY

Heard you crashed Lucia Bennett's Sweet Sixteen
last night.

ME

Oh?

I *did* crash Lucia Bennett's Sweet Sixteen, but I don't know how Tony is aware of that. Lucia goes to school in Smithtown, which is at least an hour from us. Duke, Nigel, and I pretended to be visiting from England (every girl loves a British accent). We wore matching bow ties. It was awesome.

TONY

My friend Eric was there—he's dating Lucia's older sister—and he said this guy he'd never seen before was break-dancing like nobody's business and got with this girl Michelle Kannin, who has a boyfriend in college.

ME

So you thought of me? I'm flattered.

TONY

I've seen you dance, man. You're wild. Remember the party last year?

Flashback to Huntington Cinemas' Christmas party the year before, when I filled a flask with Smirnoff, and Tony and I got so drunk that we stuck our heads into the cases of popcorn and ate until Roger made us stop.

TONY

Dude, by the way . . . have you seen the new chick?

Garrett.

ME

What about her?

TONY

She's <u>bangin'.</u> Think she'd be into me?

Something strange takes over me, a swirling in my stomach I've never felt before. I'm pretty sure it's jealousy. I don't want Tony to hit on Garrett. But why should I care? *I* don't want to date her.

TONY

You're supervising her, right? Put in a good word
for me?

ME

Uh, okay. See ya later, Tony.

I head into the lobby, where I spot Garrett, who has already taken her place behind the ticket machine. I sneak up behind her, trying not to draw any more attention to myself than necessary.

GARRETT

Hey.

ME

Oh. Hey.

Smooth, Henry. She looks silly in her uniform, but not in a bad way. In a cute way. She smells good too, like the kind of tea my father keeps in the pantry and makes if he's having trouble sleeping. Her hair is pulled back and her neck is exposed. I have the sudden urge to kiss her.

GARRETT

Did you, um, have a nice weekend?

I debate whether to tell her about the party I crashed the night before. Not because she'll be impressed (I already know she won't be; I can tell these kinds of things) but because she seems to, I don't know, actually *like* being around me, and that's dangerous. For me *and* for her.

ME

Yeah. I had sex in the backseat
of my car. It was hot.

GARRETT

(without flinching)
Did you listen to music?

ME

What?

GARRETT

While you were doing it. Did you listen
to any music?

I'm so surprised by her question that I am, momentarily,
speechless. I also lied to her; I didn't have sex. All I could
think about when I kissed Michelle was Garrett. It was . . .
weird. I drove home from the party without Duke and
Nigel (Duke brought his own car), watched *Gangs of New
York,* and fell asleep with my clothes still on.

ME

Uh, no. Do you remember how to scan a ticket?

GARRETT

Yes. I'm not stupid.

ME

I never said you were.

GARRETT

You implied it.

ME

No, I didn't.

GARRETT

All right. If you say so.

We continue working. I steal glances at her; every time I look, she looks away. She applies Chap Stick, like, ten million times. If her goal is to draw attention to her lips, it's definitely working.

GARRETT

Oh, my weekend? It was amazing—thank you so much for asking. What did I do? Well, I painted my nails and ate bonbons on Friday night. Saturday I went to a Jonas Brothers concert at Nassau

Coliseum, and I don't even <u>like</u> the Jonas Brothers
but they called me up onstage and I performed an
original song on the harpsichord, they just happened
to have one, and people threw flowers at me and
now I have my own record deal.

I can't help but laugh.

ME

Sounds eventful.

GARRETT

Yeah, it was. (Pause.) Are you really not going to ask
me how my weekend was?

ME

Let's start over. How was your weekend, Garrett?

GARRETT

Fine.

ME

You can't just say <u>fine.</u> Not after whining about it.

GARRETT

(laughing)

Okay, okay. Last night I went to the mall with the
J Squ—with Jyllian, Jessica, and London.

ME

The mall? Wow . . . you guys are wild.

GARRETT

It was fun! Honestly.

ME

How fun can the mall possibly be? There's nothing
to do except walk around.

GARRETT

We can't <u>all</u> party until three in the morning.
<u>Someone</u> has to be a little boring to make up for
your lifestyle, Mr. Arlington.

I know she's kidding, and that she's flirting with me—at
least, I *think* she's flirting with me. As much as I don't
want to like it, I do.

ME

What can I say? I like to keep things exciting.

We're interrupted by a slew of moviegoers who want to buy tickets. Garrett and I establish a kind of rhythm; before I know it, our shift is almost up. The night is almost over.

GARRETT

You don't have to keep ignoring me at school, you
know. It's not that hard to say hello.

ME

(slightly taken aback)
It's not you. I . . . I sort of keep to myself.

GARRETT

I've gathered. But you can still say <u>hello.</u> You act like
we don't even know each other.

How can I make her understand that it's better this way? That I'll only wind up hurting her if we get close because I can tell she likes me and that's what always happens to girls who like me. They get hurt.

ME

Yeah, you're right.

Garrett rests her hands on the cash register. I'm speechless at how beautiful she is. And how *cool* she is. I wonder if she's heard the rumor about us hooking up. It's all over school, or at least, it was; I don't know if anyone's talking about it anymore. I can't imagine she *wouldn't* have heard, but she hasn't brought it up, and if I know anything about women, there's no way she'd be able to bottle up all those emotions around me. Unless she's insane . . .

ME

I figured you didn't want to talk to me.

GARRETT

What?

ME

That's why I've kept my distance. Well, one of
the reasons.

GARRETT

Why would you think that?

ME

The J Squad aren't exactly my biggest fans. Now
that you're friends with them . . . I'm sure they've
filled your brain with all kinds of terrible stories.

Garrett looks right at me.

GARRETT

We don't really talk about you.

ME

Oh.

I can't tell whether I'm upset or relieved.

ME (cont.)

You know . . . I didn't have sex with that girl. From
the party last night. (Garrett is silent.) Not that you
care or that it matters at all, but in the spirit of
honesty I just thought you should know.

GARRETT

Why did you lie?

ME

I guess . . . I wanted to impress you? Or scare you
away? I honestly don't know.

GARRETT

Well, you know, thanks for telling me the truth.

ME

Sure.

GARRETT

It's good to know you're not a total man-slut.

Before I can respond, Roger approaches us and shoos us
away like we're flies.

ROGER

Time to go home! Close up the registers!

He moves toward the concession stand, and I start
counting out the money in my register.

ME

I guess, uh, I'll see you at school tomorrow?

Garrett smiles at me, an electric kind of smile that sets me off like a firecracker. It's as though the entire room has gone dark and we're the only people in it, and there's a spotlight on us and we are totally illuminated.

I see her so clearly.

"Yup," she says, and then: "I'm glad you had a nice weekend, Henry."

At home, my father is sitting at the kitchen table reading a book and eating a bowl of pasta.

ME

Any good?

He looks up from the book (*Crime and Punishment*), swallows, and nods.

DAD

Creepy.

ME

I read that in my English class last year.
I really liked it.

He goes back to eating. So many questions are left un-asked: How was your day, Henry? How are Duke and Nigel? Are you putting together your college applications? Are you lonely? Sad? Happy? Do you miss your mother?

Some people I know curse their parents for being too in-volved in their lives, for not giving them independence.

It's the opposite for me. I used to have two parents, and now, sometimes—most of the time—it feels like I have none. I decide not to wait for a question to be asked and to ask one myself. Something simple. Efficient.

ME

Interesting day?

Dad looks surprised that I'm trying to make conversa-tion. Not displeased. Just surprised.

DAD

I guess. You?

ME

Work was fine. There's a new girl.

DAD

Pretty?

ME

Yeah.

DAD

The most dangerous kind.

I give a knowing smile and continue into less stable territory. I'm not sure why I suddenly feel so bold.

ME

She reminds me of Mom, actually. In a good way.

Creases immediately form in his forehead, and his lips press themselves into a thin red line.

DAD

I'm gonna grab a beer and get to bed, kid.
Good night.

Just like that he is off.

My mother left when I was twelve and put thousands of miles between us. My father left me in a different way. He didn't put miles between us, just walls, and five years later I'm still not sure which is worse.

8

GARRETT

I am finally beginning to tell Jessica and Jyllian apart.

"I'm very knowledgeable about the things that are important to me," Jessica assured me the other day in the cafeteria. "Brangelina and *The Biggest Loser*. And the entire country of Mexico. Do you even *know* how cheap Tijuana is? I went there with my parents last summer and we survived on less than five hundred dollars. And we were there for an entire week."

"That's disgusting. I'm surprised you weren't kidnapped

and forced to smuggle drugs in your own body," London said.

"Like in *Maria Full of Grace*," I volunteered, remembering a movie my father made me watch with him in which a girl swallows tiny bags full of cocaine and crosses the border with them inside her.

Jyllian shook her head. "Maria is *such* a fugly name."

And then, of course, there's Jessica's purse—a purse that appears to have come straight out of *Mary Poppins*. It's seemingly bottomless, and the random shit she pulls out of it always keeps me on my toes. Yesterday, she removed a live salamander, and the day before, a remote control. "Just in case," she said.

Jyllian, from what I can tell, is a little minx. Guys are pretty much all she talks about. I find this interesting because her stories are obviously exaggerated, if not entirely fictional. I can't tell if Jyllian is a pathological liar or if she's one of those girls who simply exists in a completely different reality than everyone else.

Her latest piece of news? She met one of the guys from *High School Musical* at a restaurant in the city the weekend before and they hooked up in the women's bathroom.

"That should tell you something about him," London says, laughing. We're walking around the Roosevelt Field

Mall after school; there's not *that* much to do on Long Island, after all, and the mall is as good a place as any to see and be seen. I never went to a mall back in Chicago. If I needed something—a new pair of jeans, a fancy pair of underwear, a calculator—I would go to individual stores. In a civilized city. The suburbs are just so . . . "Crazy" (Patsy Cline, 1961).

We're hardly the only young people here. The entire mall (the food court in particular) is filled with kids from local high schools, London tells me as we walk. It's Monday after school. I looked for Henry during the day, but I think he was absent. "A lot of the Hofstra kids come here on the weekends." She stops to adjust her bra. "Remember, Garrett: *college guys*. They're the ones who are boyfriend material."

I avoid her gaze.

"I could have a boyfriend if I wanted one," Jyllian says to no one in particular. She has a thick scarf wrapped around her neck even though it's not cold at all. "Millions of them. I don't want one, of course. I like being single. I need my freedom."

"Sure you do," says Jessica.

"If I had a boyfriend," Jyllian says, "I couldn't have hooked up with that guy last weekend. And it was amazing, ladies. He *sang* to me. Like, his riffing was *out of control*. So lavish. And he said he could probably get me a part in the next HSM movie." She averts her eyes, staring into the window of J.Crew. "Not that I even *want* a part in the next movie. God."

"Any Ben updates?" London asks. I like London the most of the three because she's bitchy and fun and knows how to keep a conversation going. She does ask a lot of questions, though.

"I haven't called him in a while," I say, attempting to be casual about the whole thing. After all, "Love Is a Losing Game" (Amy Winehouse, 2007). "I guess it's really over."

"Good. *Don't* call him," London says, "and don't text him. Definitely don't e-mail him. And if he does contact you, don't respond. With these kinds of things, no communication is the only way to go. Cold turkey. That's how you'll get over him."

"I stopped going to his Facebook page," I say, "which has been a total blessing. Not seeing his status updates or his pictures has made me much less upset."

"That's a major step in the right direction," Jessica says.

"'Ignorance is bliss,'" Jyllian says, air-quoting with her fingers. "Whoever said that was a *genius.*"

We all get Diet Cokes at McDonald's and sit down at one of the food court's many plastic tables.

"Enough about Ben," Jessica says once we're settled. "Tell us all about Henry."

"Everything," London echoes. "Every little detail."

"Well," I say, thinking how to spin this so that my pursuit of Henry sounds interesting. "He's training me at the Huntington Cinemas, and—"

"That place is gross, by the way," Jyllian says, playing with her straw. "I went there once to see some random movie and sat on a piece of gum. It *ruined* this vintage skirt I *loved.* So rusty."

I'm slightly offended that Jyllian called the cinema gross, but I let it slide.

"What's it like working with him?" London asks. "Does he flirt with you?"

No. I think he hates me, but I also think maybe he likes me, and I can't concentrate on anything or anyone else when he's near me. "A little," I say.

Jessica giggles. "Does he *lurve* you yet?"

"Not yet," I admit.

"Why not?" London asks. Her eyebrows are perfectly arched, and her expression makes her cheekbones appear even more angular than they actually are.

"I mean, I'm getting there," I say. "I just don't want to come on too strong, you know? It's all in the timing."

"True," London says, "but you don't have much time. Destiny's Sweet Sixteen is barely a month away."

"He invited me out," I say quickly, before I can think of a different, lesser lie. I don't want the J Squad to think I'm failing. I don't want them to cut me loose.

"On a date?"

"Yep," I say.

London looks skeptical. "Where to?"

"OMG," Jyllian squeals, "is he hiring a limo service to take you into the city to one of those hole-in-the-wall restaurants in Little Italy and then to see *Mamma Mia*?"

"Um, no," I tell her.

"Oh. Too bad."

"He asked me over to . . . his house. To watch a movie."

All three of them look shocked. Intrigued. Definitely impressed.

"No shit," Jessica says. "When?"

I shrug as if it's No Big Deal. "Next weekend. After work."

(Note to self: Secure invitation to Henry's house next weekend after work.)

"I don't think any girl from school has ever been over to his house," Jyllian says, "well, except for—"

"I'm getting a stress headache," London says, massaging her temples. "I need to go home and lie down."

I drop Jyllian off first, then Jessica. Young Love's *Too Young to Fight It* is in the CD player.

"So," London says as I pull up to her house. The way the light from the street fills the car gives her an ethereal look, as if she's slightly more than human. I am both excited and terrified by the prospect of her friendship.

"So."

"I can't believe Henry asked you over."

"I know. Me either."

"It's a really big deal, you know."

"Is it?"

"Yes," she says. The way her voice resonates makes me feel like nothing in the world is more important than my going over to Henry's house next weekend. I start to get nervous.

"Good, I guess."

London gives me a smile as though it were a present. "You really might get him to go out with you, Garrett. Kudos."

I think this is supposed to be a compliment, but it makes me uneasy. "Did you think that I *wouldn't* be able to?"

"Just make sure you get him to take you to Destiny's

Sweet Sixteen," London says. "Nobody likes a failure." Then she kisses me once on each cheek. "And be careful. Thanks for the ride."

I want to ask *why* I should be careful but, before I can, she's gone.

I avoid my parents and head straight to my room. They're curled up on the sofa in our den watching TV. If I say hello, they'll want me to hang out with them, and I'm not in the mood. I don't feel like being the third wheel with a loving couple, even if that couple is my parents. Actually, even more so *because* they're my parents. Gross.

My room is in various stages of unpacked. There are still boxes full of books and trinkets and pictures. Some—not all—of my clothes are folded away. The only thing perfectly in place is my CD collection, which I've arranged and sorted alphabetically. While most people buy their music on iTunes (or download it illegally), I like having something to hold in my hand. I also have a bunch of vocal selections I can *sort of* play on the guitar; mostly, I read through the lyrics of my favorite songs the way some people flip through magazines.

I take out my cell phone and dial Amy back in Chicago. With the time difference, she should just be getting home from school. It goes straight to voice mail. I leave this message: "Hey, stranger. It's been a long time since we've spoken. What gives? I hope school is fun, but not *too* fun, and that you miss me every day and cry yourself to sleep at night because you can't live without me. You better have a kick-ass reason for not getting back to me, okay? Call me."

When I hang up I think, *That was pathetic,* but that's the thing about best friends—you're allowed to sound pathetic because they love you unconditionally. Or at least, they're supposed to.

I check my e-mail (one from my English teacher about our *Hamlet* assignment and one advertising penile enlargement surgery) and watch an episode of *30 Rock* on Hulu. Then my thoughts turn to Ben and "The Day We Fell Apart" (Kelly Clarkson, 2009). I really did think that I would hear from him by now. That he would miss me enough to call. How could I have been so wrong?

When I close my eyes, I see him. *Ben.* Lying on my bed. His hair is disheveled and his eyes are sleepy and his lips are opened slightly. His shirt is crumpled on the floor and his chest seems like this enormous wall of muscle and flesh; I rest my head there and let my hands travel across his stomach. It's the end of June. School is over for the year and my parents are away for the weekend; they have specifically asked me *not* to have any guests over, but Ben is not a guest (even though I am sure they would disagree). Ben is my boyfriend. Ben is "My Superman" (Santogold, 2008).

"What are you thinking about?" he asks me. His fingers hesitate slightly when they reach the material of my bra, then crawl like spiders across the black cotton.

"You," I say. He moves on top of me, resting his weight on his elbows, and kisses me, soft, lovely kisses on my lips and earlobes and neck. When I touch him I imagine that this is what it feels like to place your hand in a fire. I am burning.

Paolo Nutini is singing on my computer, and my iTunes is playing a light show; the colors bounce off Ben in muted reds and blues and greens and yellows. I close my eyes to savor this moment, these few seconds of stillness before the inevitable *what comes next*, only when I open them I no longer see Ben. I see Henry. *His* strong arms are around me. His beautiful eyes are staring right into mine.

"What are you doing here?" I ask him.

"What do you think?" He leans forward to kiss me—

"Garrett! Are you in there?"

My mother's voice wakes me, and I realize I'm in my bed. Alone. I look at my clock—it's not even eight p.m.

"I didn't know you were home," she says after I open the bedroom door. She is holding a tiny bottle of scented lotion from Bath & Body Works and the latest *Teen Vogue*. "Want me to give you a hand massage and gossip about underage celebrities?"

"Uh, maybe later."

She looks disappointed. "Okay, sweetie. I'll be downstairs, probably doing Downward Facing Dog."

She leaves, and I am *livid* with my subconscious for allowing Henry to invade my memory. How dare he. I don't love Henry. I love Ben. Well, I used to. Now . . . who knows. But I certainly don't want to get naked with Henry Arlington anytime soon. That much I know for sure.

I need to step up my game. Prove to the J Squad that I can seduce Henry without falling for him, and prove to myself that I can be the one in control, the one who doesn't get hurt. I'll start by securing an invitation to his house for next weekend. It will happen. I simply need to figure out *how*.

PINK LYRICS RUNNING THROUGH MY HEAD AS I FIGURE OUT A PLAN

"I'm comin' up so you better get this party started."
—*Get the Party Started*

"I hope I don't end up in jail." —*Tonight's the Night*

"Nine, eight, seven, six, five, four, three, two, one, fun." —*Funhouse*

I have an idea. I go downstairs to my father's study; he's also still in the middle of unpacking, but has stuffed his bookshelves with his favorite books (on film studies) and DVDs. I may not particularly care about the Greatest Movies of All Time, but Henry does, and that's how I'm going to get him. And I *am* going to get him. Just wait and see.

The next morning, at school, Henry stops at my locker.

"Hey," he says. He's wearing a red polo shirt and a tight pair of khakis. He looks good.

"Hey," I say back, surprised that he's paying attention to me. I glance around for the J Squad, hoping they're watching.

"Just saying hello and not *ignoring you*." The way he says it makes me remember our conversation over the weekend at work.

"Thanks," I say. "Are you feeling better?"

"Hmm?"

"Yesterday. You were out sick, right?"

"You noticed?"

I'm suddenly embarrassed. I want him to think I'm interested in him—that's the whole point, of course—but not that I follow his every move. "It was oddly silent," I say. "Not a single girl cried all day, so I figured you weren't around."

He laughs, and I can tell that was the right answer.

"Well," he says, smiling, "see you later, Garrett."

I watch him leave, walking slowly down the senior hallway.

Henry said hello to me, and I made him laugh.

Game on.

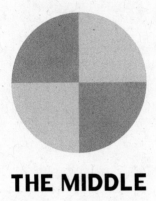

THE MIDDLE

Love is a temporary madness. It erupts like an earthquake and then subsides. And when it subsides you have to make a decision. You have to work out whether your roots have so entwined together that it is inconceivable that you should ever part.

—from *Captain Corelli's Mandolin* (2001)

9

HENRY

INT.—MY BEDROOM, FRIDAY NIGHT

I'd rather talk to people on the computer than in person. In person you have to make eye contact and pretend you're actually interested in the conversation. You have to (attempt to) complete your sentences and move the muscles in your face to feign emotion. This is something I'm terrible at. Most people think I'm distant because I assume I'm better than they are, but that's not it at all. I'm distant because I can't relate, because being around them makes me uncomfortable. This is why I love the Internet. It's difficult to be detached one-on-one, but AIM makes it easy.

> **TheDuke69:** dude . . . skip work and come party
> **Enrico2000:** no can do
> **TheDuke69:** all work and no play . . .
> **Enrico2000:** someone's gotta pay the billz
> **TheDuke69:** u don't have any billz
> **Enrico2000:** you know what i mean
> **TheDuke69:** no i don't
> **TheDuke69:** saw u talking 2 Garrett 2day

Shit. I thought I'd been totally stealth. It's not anything major—anything other than *hello*—but every day since Tuesday, I've stopped to acknowledge her presence and prove I'm not a complete asshole. Has anyone else besides Duke noticed?

> **TheDuke69:** u there?
> **Enrico2000:** yeah
> **TheDuke69:** n e thing i should know about?
> **Enrico2000:** nope

TheDuke69: ur not like . . . dating her behind our backs, rite? i've never seen u talk 2 a girl u didn't wanna hook up with b4. unless . . . u wanna get with her again?

Again? How about a first time?

Enrico2000: it's nothing like that, okay?
TheDuke69: u would tell me if there was something going on, rite?
Enrico2000: of course

I feel bad lying to Duke, but then again . . . am I really lying? Nothing's going on between Garrett and me. Not yet, at least. Even if there were something to report, Duke and Nigel certainly wouldn't approve, so what's the point of saying anything at all?

TheDuke69: when do u get off tonight?
Enrico2000: around 11 or so
TheDuke69: call me l8r. meet me & N at this girl's party in Sea Cliff. Should be krazy!
Enrico2000: OK OK . . . i gotta go. Duty calls
TheDuke69: lata, playa

INT.–HUNTINGTON CINEMAS

I get to work early. I'm already wearing my uniform, and I brought a change of clothes in case I decide to meet up with Duke and Nigel. Lately, I haven't been hanging out with them as much. I don't necessarily feel bad about this—life happens—but I do miss their company. Being friends with D & N is easy; they don't expect me to chime in with some incredible insight about shit I don't care about. They get that I live on Planet Henry most of the time, and leave me alone as long as I let them visit occasionally.

I check in with Roger, who has me count out one of the cash registers and then heads back to his office.

Garrett isn't here yet, and I relish the time alone. It seems odd that our schedules are more or less the same, but I don't press her (or Roger) about it. I don't actually *mind* working with her. I'm bothered by my feelings for her, sure, and it would be easier if she weren't around . . . but there is something that I undeniably like about her. She's the first girl I've met who isn't afraid to tell me how it is. I appreciate that. Girls who agree with everything I say aren't worth my time. Where's the challenge?

I recognize a few chicks from school waiting in line to buy tickets for one of the foreign films, *Eso No Es Mi*

Sombrero (*That Is Not My Hat*). They smile at me. I smile back. One of them is cute: short brown hair, clear skin, nice teeth. A freshman.

ME

Hey. You go to East Shore, right?

CUTE FRESHMAN

(nodding)

You're Henry Arlington.

ME

That's what they tell me.

CUTE FRESHMAN

(laughing)

Well, um, one for . . . the Spanish movie.

She glances back at her friends, all of whom have turned a bright, embarrassing pink. I'm about to tell her that the ticket is free (just don't tell my boss) when someone behind me says: "That'll be eleven fifty."

Garrett.

I turn around and man, she looks hot. Damn. The freshman pales in comparison.

CUTE FRESHMAN

I have a student ID.

GARRETT

Good for you. Just saved yourself a dollar.

The rest of the girls pay for their tickets and hurry into the theater.

ME

You sure know how to scare people away.

GARRETT

I have a lot of practice.

What I like about working the register is that, if it's a busy night, time really flies by. I don't know whether Garrett recognizes that I'm being standoffish, but since she isn't exactly initiating conversation either, I figure she's aware. It's better this way. Even if we got together it wouldn't end well. Plus, it's not like we have *that* much in common. She's from Chicago, and I'm from Long Island. Enough said.

Garrett takes a break and comes back with a fountain soda. She sips from the straw, watching me as though I'm supposed to say something.

ME

You're doing a great job.

GARRETT

Thanks.

I look at my watch: 10:06. It's weird, being here with Garrett. We're not friends, but we're no longer strangers. I'm unsure how to act around her. Saying hello at school is one thing; standing next to her, so close we're practically touching, and trying to sustain dialogue is another thing entirely.

ME

Uh, who do you have for English?

GARRETT

Jacobs. Why?

ME

Oh, I have Smythe. I hear Jacobs is a real piece of work. Like, really nuts.

GARRETT

She's kooky, but I appreciate it. Keeps
things interesting.

ME

What are you guys reading?

GARRETT

The Inferno. You?

ME

Oh, we read that already. We're reading
Heart of Darkness.

GARRETT

I didn't like that one.

ME

Why not?

GARRETT

I mean, it was fine, but I'm not typically a fan of
story-within-a-story kind of books.

ME

Me either! Well, I don't read a whole lot, but in
movies . . . I hate that.

GARRETT

Ugh, I know. Except for—

BOTH

<u>Forrest Gump</u>!

We both laugh.

ME

So, uh, did you have a nice week?

GARRETT

It was all right. I'm still adjusting to East Shore. It's
really different than my last high school.

ME

How so?

GARRETT

The people are just, I don't know . . . more intense.

ME

Yeah, well, I doubt <u>anyone</u> is more intense than the
girls you've been hanging out with.

Garrett doesn't respond; I wonder if I pissed her off by
mentioning the J Squad. But then she looks at me, really
looks at me, and I find it impossible to turn away. I don't
see her from a distance, like she's playing a role in a film
or anything like that—she is right here.

"Thanks for saying hi to me this week," she says. "It
was really sweet of you."

I totally clam up. My forehead gets sweaty, and I scratch
the back of my neck. I don't know if I'm ready for this.
What does she want from me, exactly?

"Do you have any crazy weekend plans?" she asks.

ME

Not really.

I remember how easy it was to talk to Garrett when I
first met her. Then I close my eyes and squeeze until the
memory bursts and I am back to my life, where things are
never easy. It is 10:11. Just under an hour left.

We finish at the same time and walk to the break room, where all the lockers are. There's also a box of coffee and a few stale donuts on a table in the corner. I take off my uniform (is she watching me?) and put on the shirt I brought with me. I'm about to open my phone and text Duke for the address of the party when Garrett's bag tips over. All the contents spill in front of me.

GARRETT

Shit. I'm sorry.

She begins to pick everything up in such a hurry that I wonder if there's something incredibly personal on the floor, like a tampon or birth control pills or a picture of her dry-humping a tree. I bend over to help; when I see what was in her bag, my heart jumps.

Movies.

I feel like a kid in a candy store. *An American in Paris. Dr. Strangelove. Annie Hall. The Crying Game.*

ME

Are these yours?

GARRETT

Yeah. I like to make sure I have something good to watch in case I get bored.

I know exactly what she means. Not having a DVD on me at all times—in my locker, in my car, wherever—is one of the scariest things I can think of.

ME

Have you seen all of these?

GARRETT

Like a million times each. Except for <u>Annie Hall.</u> I've only seen it once. I'm in the middle of watching it a second time.

ME

Do you like it?

GARRETT

Yeah. It's different than a lot of movies that were made in the seventies. I think it's one of Woody Allen's best.

ME

What do you like about it?

My question seems to ignite her.

GARRETT

Well, for starters I love Diane Keaton. I love Woody,
too, and how it was made, you know? How so much
of the movie is just talking. How the characters
break the fourth wall and speak directly to the
camera—it makes the whole thing feel intimate and
personal, like I'm part of it.

The more she talks, the faster my heart beats. It's as if
she's a painting and every word is a brushstroke, coloring
her in until she is complete.

"It's nice to just watch a scene in a movie without so
much cutting back and forth between the actors," Garrett
says. "Makes it seem more like real life." She laughs. "I
must have just bored the hell out of you."

"No," I tell her. "No. You didn't."

I cannot believe how she talks about movies. How she
thinks about them.

Like I do.

"What are you doing right now?"

She narrows her eyes. "What do you mean?"

I point at the stack of DVDs in her hands. "You said
you're in the middle of *Annie Hall.* If you're not doing anything . . . maybe you'd want to come over to my house and
watch it?"

147

"You want me to come over to your house?"

My cheeks feel hot. "I mean, you don't have to. I just have a really big bed that's good to watch movies on. I mean, a really big TV." I smack my forehead. "Sorry. I should get going."

"No," she says, placing her hand on my arm. I practically jump at her touch. "I'd like to come over. That sounds . . . nice."

Nice. "Uh, okay." What have I just done? There's no time to prepare. This is going to be a disaster.

Yet, I am excited. Nervous. Thrilled. Ready to puke.

I decide against texting Duke—he'll only bother me with a million questions.

"I have my car with me, so I'll just follow you?" Garrett asks.

I cannot form words. I simply nod and walk straight ahead, out of the break room and into the parking lot. Garrett is beside me. She goes over to her car, and maybe it's the way the light from the street hits her face, or maybe it's the way she moves, or maybe it has nothing to do with her at all and the change is happening somewhere deep inside me, but for the first time in a long time I feel, I don't know, alive.

10

GARRETT

Who knew that a couple of perfectly selected DVDs and a monologue about Woody Allen would help me worm my way into Henry Arlington's heart?

Oh, that's right.

Me.

Which is why I'm standing in the middle of his living room, just before Friday night becomes Saturday morning, about to go upstairs to his bedroom.

Take *that*, J Squad.

I look around; pictures of Henry at various ages stand

everywhere like "Statues" (Foo Fighters, 2007). There's a long leather couch, a few vases with dried flowers, a gorgeous grand piano, and some interesting framed posters on the wall.

I follow Henry into the kitchen and watch him pull two beers from the fridge. "Take whatever you want," he says, motioning to the pantry. I open it and find a smorgasbord of chips and cookies; I grab some Oreos and raise them in silent victory. Henry laughs and together we go upstairs, into his room.

Henry's room is not what I expect. It's pretty minimal. His bed is against the wall, and opposite it is a large flat-screen TV atop an elegant black dresser. Next to that is a glass desk with an oversized Apple monitor; on either side of the desk is a rectangular speaker sitting on a narrow stand. His walls are stark white. There's a framed picture of Elvis Costello and three enormous windows that overlook his backyard. A tiny nightstand with a lamp. A navy blue bean bag chair next to his closet. Oh, yes—and there are DVDs. Hundreds of them. Three bookshelves that stretch from floor to ceiling, and they're packed.

So this is where Henry sleeps. This is where he lives.

"We'll have to keep the volume kinda low—I don't want to wake up my dad."

"Where's your mom?" I ask.

Henry flinches. It's a slight reaction, but I notice it nonetheless. "She's dead."

"Oh," I say, immediately regretting my question. "I'm so sorry, Henry. I had no idea."

He shrugs. "It's okay." He opens a beer and passes it to me. It's tangy and sweet. "Ever had Tsingtao?"

I'm not a huge drinker in general, but I do like this. "Nope. It's really good, though."

"My dad is kind of a beer connoisseur," he says. "He usually has the fridge stocked with stuff I didn't even know existed. He doesn't care if I have one or two, as long as I'm not driving." He looks at me. "So, actually, you shouldn't be drinking that. If you're gonna drive home."

Is he suggesting I should stay the night? I put the beer down. "You're right."

"Unless you *want* to drink. Then I won't, and I can drive you home."

"That's okay," I tell him. "But thanks."

"I still can't believe you're such a film fanatic. I thought when you took the job at Huntington, well, that you were—"

"Lying?"

"Yeah. Sorry."

"You don't have to apologize. My father is a film professor, so I've grown up with an appreciation for truly great movies. And truly *bad* ones."

He laughs and says, "Wow." Usually when I tell people what my dad does they think it's interesting, but it's never a big deal. To Henry, though, it really is.

"Getting to study and watch and talk about films every day sounds like a dream come true," he says, kicking off his sneakers. He's wearing white socks that cut off just below the ankle, and his jeans are tattered in all the right places.

"I guess," I say, slipping out of my own shoes. I sit on the edge of his bed. "Maybe you should become a professor."

"Nah," he says, taking another sip of his beer. "I like to keep to myself. If you haven't already noticed."

I have.

"I'd like to write movies. To be a screenwriter, you know? I just really want to be a part of them. A part of something that'll last a whole lot longer than I will." He blushes. I doubt he's ever said those words out loud before. "That must sound so corny."

"Not at all," I tell him. "It's good to have a goal, and clearly you know a lot about film. Do you write a lot?"

"Some. Not much."

"That's too bad."

"Why?"

"You seem like someone who has stories to tell."

He smiles an I'm-embarrassed kind of smile. "So what do you want to do with your life?" he asks.

This is going to sound ridiculous, but I have absolutely no answer. And truthfully, it's the first time anyone (other than my parents) has asked me this question. When Henry speaks about screenwriting, there's real *passion* there. I don't have anything I feel that way about. Except music.

"I don't know," I say.

"You must want to do *something*. Candy striper? Go-go dancer?"

"No, I mean . . . I don't know what I want to do. I honestly have no idea."

Henry rubs his chin. "Why do you think that is?"

"What do you mean?"

"I'm not trying to make you feel bad," he says, "it's just that most people have *some* idea what they want to do when they grow up. And if you don't, I guess I'm curious why."

I flash a smile. "Are you sure you don't want to be a therapist?"

"Definitely," Henry says. "I can barely deal with my own issues, let alone other people's." He sits down next to me.

"So. Spill. If you could do anything in the world, what would it be? And you have to answer."

I try to think of something impressive-sounding. Doctor? No. Lawyer? No. Executive producer of a reality TV show? Maybe. But no.

"You're taking too long. What's on the tip of your tongue? Just say it. I won't judge you."

Somehow, I believe him. "I'd want to work in the music industry," I say.

"Doing what?"

"Maybe producing albums, or writing lyrics, or helping discover new artists."

The words leave my mouth and I think, *Whoa. Where did that come from?* I've never really thought about music in terms of a career. Okay, that's not exactly true. I have thought about it, just never seriously. I'm not good enough to be a recording artist, but why couldn't I find some other way to be involved in the industry? Why did it take Henry's asking me point-blank to make me admit this desire?

"That's awesome," Henry says, sliding his hand over my knee and squeezing. His touch feels "Wonderful" (The Beach Boys, 1967).

Then I freeze. What am I doing? I shouldn't be talking about this kind of stuff with him. I don't actually want to *date* him. I want to *play* him. I try to ignore the fact that we seem to have incredible chemistry and when I'm around him, all thoughts of Ben are completely gone. I remember how Henry lied to people about us hooking up, and how many hearts he's broken in the past. I remember my desire to be the one in control. It's time to take my plan to the next level.

I'm still wearing my Huntington Cinemas uniform; in my bag is a low-cut long-sleeved shirt and a pair of jeans. "Do you mind if I change?"

"Go for it," he says.

I follow his directions to the bathroom and close the door behind me. I change at a leisurely pace. I remind myself I don't want a boyfriend—*especially* not Henry Arlington. I shake my hair out and fix my eyeliner where it's smudged. I study myself in the mirror. I wonder what Henry sees when he looks at me.

When I return, I flick off the overhead light. "Ready for the movie?" I ask. Henry inserts the DVD into his computer, which is hooked up to his TV. I crawl to the far side of his bed. Is it weird to lie down on his pillow? I'm not sure. I do it anyway.

"We can watch it from the beginning if you want."

"Nah," he says, pressing Play and getting on the bed with me. "I know this one pretty much by heart."

The moment feels incredibly intimate even though we

aren't touching. I can smell him on the comforter and in the air surrounding me; I never realized that Henry has a smell, but he does. It's intoxicating and completely indescribable. It's just *him*.

We're at the part when Diane Keaton and Woody Allen have split up for the first time but then she calls him to kill a bug in her apartment and they get back together. I think about the time my mom found a colony of bees living in our basement in Chicago—she started crying and called 911. Then I think about the time I was home alone and found a roach in the kitchen, and made Ben come over and kill it. The thing I love about this movie is how it's funny and sad at the same time, how very much like *life* it is.

Somehow, while we're watching, Henry and I move closer. We're not on top of each other or anything, but first my leg, then his, my foot, then his, my arm, then his, slowly inch together. When we finally touch, it's magical. The invisible hairs on my arms are shocked; my skin tingles and my blood flows more easily.

By the end, we're overlapping. Neither one of us moves even though the credits are rolling.

"So," he says, breaking the silence. "Better the second time around?"

"Yeah," I say, my hand resting in the middle of his chest. I think: *All that is between my skin and his skin is a thin layer of cotton.* It's been a few weeks since I've touched a boy; I remember how much I love it. Being held. Holding someone. "Do you think they should have wound up together?" I ask. "Alvy and Annie?"

"I don't know."

"Well, what do you think?"

"I think, you know, love is . . . complicated. And scary."

"Why scary?"

"Maybe scary isn't the right word," he says. The room is dark; all I can see are his eyes. "More like terrifying."

I laugh. "I'll second that."

We stay this way for what seems like a very long time. I'm confused by tonight's discovery: a side of Henry Arlington that I never knew existed, a side that was hinted at the first time I met him but had yet to expose itself again until now. And even though I know the J Squad would be *very* disappointed in me if they knew I was in Henry's arms, in Henry's bed, and nothing happened between us—and, frankly, I'm disappointed with myself—I can't bring myself to make a move. I silently curse Henry for making my plan more difficult than I imagined.

"Do you think it would be better if they'd never met?" Henry asks. "Then he wouldn't have to go through the heartache of getting rejected. Of seeing her with someone new. It's awful to have someone who's, like, your entire world for so long and then have her disappear from your life completely. I can't imagine anything worse."

I want to ask if he is talking about his mother. He must be.

"You're right," I say, "but if they'd never met then he wouldn't have gotten the chance to experience loving her. Love is the most powerful emotion there is. And in the end, he's grateful for that."

"Is he?"

"Yeah," I tell Henry, "I think so."

"It doesn't work out, though. Their relationship was a failure."

"Just because two people don't wind up spending their entire lives together doesn't mean their relationship was a failure."

Henry is silent. Finally, he says: "I guess. . . ."

"I think that's sort of the point of the movie," I say. "That love is terrifying and hard and awful but it's also amazing and beautiful, and there's something about us, as humans, that wants that perfect relationship even though we know it's probably unattainable, and even if we *do* manage to get it, holding on to it, helping it grow into something that will last a lifetime, well . . . it's daunting in its impossibility. At least, that's how my dad describes it."

"Your dad must be really smart."

"He is," I say, and then: "But we still want it." I wonder if I am trying to convince Henry or myself of this.

"Want what?"

"Love."

He turns his head and our noses touch. He is so close. "Maybe we do."

His breath warms my face, and he pulls me closer. He is about to kiss me. And even though this is a good thing—the next step in getting Henry to call me his girlfriend and take me to Destiny's Sweet Sixteen, in getting the J Squad to induct me as a legitimate member—that I *want* him to kiss me is a bad thing, and what's going to make this all the more difficult in the end.

HENRY

INT.–EAST SHORE HIGH SCHOOL, MONDAY MORNING

School is different now. I've never worried what a girl thinks about me *post*–hooking up.

The feeling is nerve-wracking.

Exhilarating.

Paralyzing.

DUKE

So, dude, no explanation?

Duke and Nigel are standing at my locker. They're pissed I didn't meet them at the party on Friday. Right now they are mirror images of each other: arms crossed, backs straight, faces scrunched.

ME

I told you. I fell asleep.

NIGEL

For real?

ME

Yes. Why don't you guys believe me?

I take all the books I'll need for the next few periods. Then I shut my locker and start walking to class.

NIGEL

You didn't return our calls all weekend. Did you screen us? Because if you did, that's just . . . nasty.

ME

I didn't screen you. I was busy.

DUKE

You're acting weird.

ME

What? No I'm not.

NIGEL

Yes. You are.

ME

How so?

NIGEL

You're smiling, for one.

I am?

DUKE

You look, I dunno. Happy.

ME

I don't know what you guys are talking about. I'm
exactly the same as I was before the weekend.

Only I'm not. I feel like one of those Russian dolls you
take the top off and there's another, smaller doll beneath
it. The outside of me is the same, but the inside . . .

NIGEL

No, dude. You're definitely not.

ME

Well, so what if I'm happy? Is that such a crime?

DUKE

No. It's just not <u>you.</u> You're Henry Arlington. Tall.
Brooding. Man-slut.

ME

Wow, such compliments.

NIGEL

Is it a girl?

My stomach lurches, but they can't possibly suspect that anything is actually going on between Garrett and me. Can they? I haven't even told them that she works at the movie theater.

DUKE

Is it <u>her</u>?

I assume that Duke is referring to Garrett, and our IM conversation on Friday. I shake my head.

ME

What makes you think that?

A look passes between Duke and Nigel that I don't exactly understand. I know I'll have to tell them about Garrett at some point, but right now—while things are still fresh and exciting—I don't feel like opening myself up to their criticism.

DUKE

Whatever it is, dude, snap out of it. We need you in
top crasher form for Destiny's Sweet Sixteen.
You're still in, right?

Destiny's party is the upper echelon of Sweet Sixteens. It's going to be filmed by MTV, and pretty much anyone who's anyone will be in attendance. The three of us will get invites, for sure, but it's not about getting in the door. Not for us. It's what happens *afterward* that matters. What we're going to do that will guarantee a debacle of epic proportions broadcast on national television.

We've pulled a few pranks before at other parties, but

nothing major. Usually the plan is to *not* draw attention to ourselves and simply have a good time. This time, though, is different. Not only is the event for a girl at our school, but there'll be an actual television crew recording everything; eventually, the whole country will see what happens (at least, whoever tunes in will). Destiny's Sweet Sixteen is not about blending in—it's about standing out.

Duke, Nigel, and I have been hyping up this party for months. At this point, there's no way I can tell them I'm not really into it anymore without losing their friendship (and their respect).

ME
Of course.

DUKE
Sweet. We need a major planning session this week. This shit needs to be <u>hard-core.</u>

The bell rings, and I'm a few feet away from homeroom.

ME
All right. Let's talk about it later.

Duke and Nigel salute me, and I begin the day.

I can't think about anything—or anyone—other than Garrett all morning. I have never had a single person take up so much space in my brain. I scribble her initials in my notebooks and remember the softness of her body and how we talked about movies for hours and didn't fall asleep until six in the morning. The only women I have ever daydreamed about this much are Britney Spears (before she had kids) and my mother (after she left, but not in a sexual way); clearly, this thing with Garrett is new territory for me.

Before lunch, I slip a note inside Garrett's locker asking her to meet me in the courtyard. I could text her, but this note-in-locker thing seems romantically old-fashioned, and that's the kind of mood I'm in.

The courtyard at East Shore is pretty self-contained—as, by definition, courtyards are. It's still warmish outside, and some people choose to eat lunch out here instead of in the cafeteria. Most seniors go out to Wendy's or Taco Bell or this bagel place a little farther away, but I hate rushing around.

I sit on a wooden bench and wait. I wonder if she's going

to stand me up. It's one thing to be friendly at the movie theater, or in the privacy of my house, but being seen in public together is a big step. I'm willing to give it a shot, though, and see what happens. Risk the wrath of Duke and Nigel. I don't know if she's happy about the fact that we hooked up, or upset. Maybe a little of both.

I've never worried about what a girl wants before.

"Hey there."

I look up. It's Garrett.

"I got your note. I thought it was some kind of joke."

"Nope," I say. "Sit down."

I make room for her. She's wearing a red cotton sweater and a pair of jeans, and resting a brown paper bag on her lap.

"Why would you think it was a joke?" I ask.

She shrugs. "You usually eat lunch with Duke and Nigel. You guys may as well have No Girls Allowed signs taped to your backs."

"Nah," I say, "it's not like that."

"It's not?"

I think for a minute. She's got a point. "It doesn't *have* to be like that. Besides, your lunch table isn't exactly inviting either."

It's sunny out, and Garrett squints at me. Is she going to bring up the weekend? Pretend it never happened? Does she think we're dating now? She holds her hand over her eyes, blocking the light. "So the courtyard is what—neutral territory?"

"I never thought of it like that," I say, laughing, "but yeah. I guess it is."

We sit there, staring at each other. Some younger girls are clustered a few feet away, and they glance in our direction. I recognize one or two guys from my Spanish class sitting on the grass. At the other end of the courtyard, a bunch of freshmen are playing wall ball.

"So what's for lunch?" I ask. I decide not to mention our make-out session. If she wants to talk about it, she'll say something. At least, I *think* she will.

"Oh"—she opens the bag and takes out a sandwich—"turkey, lettuce, and tomato on white bread. Nothing special." She opens a bottle of water. "So. You and me," she says. "Together in public. What will people think?"

I take out my own sandwich. Roast beef with ketchup. "I dunno," I say, taking a bite. "But I don't care if you don't."

For a moment we are simply two people, sitting on a bench. Eating. Duke and Nigel are nowhere in sight; neither are London or Jessica or Jyllian. It feels good to just *eat* with a girl. No false pretenses. No tricks or gimmicks or wondering how to avoid her when she Facebooks me the next day. At some point we'll have to figure out exactly what is going on between us, but for now we can just *be*.

"Nope," she says. "I don't care at all."

And then, for no reason at all, I lean forward and kiss her cheek.

"What was that for?"

"Just because," I say. "Is that okay?"

"Sure."

"Oh, before I forget." I take out a bag with a warm chocolate chip cookie I bought in the cafeteria. "For you."

Garrett breaks off a piece of the cookie and tastes it. "Delicious," she says. "Thank you."

I slide closer and rest my hand on her leg. "You know, there's no going back now," I tell her.

"What do you mean?"

"People are going to start talking now that we've gone public. There are no secrets at East Shore."

She looks contemplative. Eventually, she says, "So? Let them talk."

I can't tell if it's from the sun or from her, but I feel my entire face light up.

Later, Duke and Nigel convince me to crash a Sweet Sixteen in Carle Place. I'm not sure why anyone would throw a party on a school night, but Duke heard about it from his mom, who takes yoga with the birthday girl's mother on Saturday mornings at the JCC.

The girl's name is Marge, and her Sweet Sixteen theme is Broadway! (I added the exclamation point.)

I'm not particularly interested in going, but I *did* ditch Duke and Nigel over the weekend and this'll make it up to them. Besides, I can't lie: watching *Annie Hall* with Garrett, talking about relationships, eating lunch in the courtyard . . . everything is moving kinda fast. I wonder how soon it will spin out of control.

Slowing things down for a night with the guys sounds pretty good.

Duke picks me up around eight. Nigel is already in the car, and I hop in the back. I'm wearing a black dress shirt and a pair of slacks. Duke is in an electric blue tuxedo, and Nigel is wearing a gray suit (and a yarmulke).

ME

'Sup?

DUKE

Nada, dude. Glad you could make it.

NIGEL

How's it hangin', Enrico?

ME

Fine, fine. So what's the plan?

Duke turns down the radio.

DUKE

Here's what I'm thinking: we're visiting from
somewhere like Kansas or Oklahoma, and we've
never been to New York before.

NIGEL

I like it. I'm definitely in the mood to say "y'all."

DUKE

I feel that.

ME

That's fine, except the theme of the party is
Broadway. Won't it be funnier if we say we're actors
or something?

NIGEL

Definitely. Broadway shows are usually dark on
Monday nights, so that would explain why we're not
in the city.

DUKE

What show should we say we're in? Should we all
be in the same show, or different ones?

I don't know a lot about musicals or Broadway in general.
I have seen *The Phantom of the Opera,* though, so that's what
I suggest.

NIGEL

Shit! I should have brought my Phantom mask.

DUKE

Why do you have a Phantom mask?

NIGEL

Why <u>don't</u> you have a Phantom mask?

DUKE

Good point.

NIGEL

Aren't we a little young to be in <u>Phantom</u>? Maybe
we should say we're in that show
<u>Spring Awakening.</u>

DUKE

Dude, that closed a while ago.

Nigel and I both shoot him looks.

DUKE (cont.)

What? My mom really likes musicals. Give me

a break.

We arrive at Chateau Briand, a popular catering hall on Long Island. The valet parks Duke's car, and we head inside. It's cocktail hour, which is out on the patio. Everything is very bright. There are palm trees (how did they get those here?), dozens of tables and chairs, and a long buffet table decorated with appetizers.

A waiter nods and says: "Welcome to the oasis."

DUKE

What did that mean?

NIGEL

I dunno. I want some shrimp. Anyone coming

with me?

ME

I will.

Duke wanders over to a table of Sweet Sixteeners doused in makeup and hair spray. The name he's chosen for tonight is Marcello.

NIGEL

What do you think his chances are?

Nigel and I grab some cheese along with some thinly sliced roast beef.

ME

With one of those girls? Not sure.

Pretty low, I'd guess.

NIGEL

Ladies do love actors, though. At least,

that's what I hear.

ME

True. But I think that pertains to, like, movie stars.

Not people in <u>Phantom of the Opera.</u>

NIGEL

And we're not even really <u>in</u> it.

ME

Touché.

We continue picking at the food. Eventually the crowd starts filtering inside. A bunch of teens have stayed in the "oasis," whatever that means; Nigel and I are chatting with two girls who go to school in Roslyn, which isn't too far from us. They're both pretty cute. The girl I'm talking to is named Desiree.

DESIREE

That must be a really demanding schedule, going to NYU School of Medicine <u>and</u> being in a Broadway show.

ME

Yeah, well . . . I make it work. That's what you do when you're passionate about something.

DESIREE

Being smart and talented is so . . . sexy.
It's such a blessing.

ME

Thanks. Although most of the time
it feels like a curse.

DESIREE

What kind of doctor do you want to be?

NIGEL
(chiming in)
He wants to be a proctologist.

I smack the back of his head.

ME

Shut up, Horatio.

DESIREE

What's that?

ME

Oh, he's kidding. Horatio thinks he has a great
sense of humor.

The other girl, Annabelle, leans forward and sips from
her Diet Coke.

ANNABELLE

A proctologist is a butt doctor.

There's a bit of uncomfortable silence, which Nigel eventually breaks by taking out a rum-filled flask.

NIGEL

Do you ladies wanna spice up your drinks?

ANNABELLE

No thanks. We have a chem test in the morning.

Desiree moves closer to me and rests her head on my shoulder. I put my arm around her and try not to think about Garrett. Nigel attempts to mimic me, but Annabelle glares at him so ferociously that he almost falls out of his chair.

I'm about to suggest to Desiree that we find somewhere a little more "private" to hang out when I hear banshee-like howling coming from inside the lobby. I glance at Nigel and raise an eyebrow.

DESIREE

What's going on in there?

NIGEL

Let's check it out.

The screaming is growing louder. Inside, the party is in full swing; a girl is standing in the middle of the dance floor, practically convulsing. Barely a foot away from her is Duke, his face frozen in fear.

ME

(whispering)

We've gotta get Duke and get outta here.

At first, I think we're in huge trouble, but the closer I get the more I realize that the girl—who I can tell is the birthday girl, Marge, by her silver tiara—isn't freaking out for a negative reason (such as finding out that we crashed her party). Rather, something is making her incredibly . . . happy.

MARGE

OMG OMG OM-EFFING-G!!! THERE IS A REAL
LIVE BROADWAY STAR AT MY PARTY!!!

Oh shit.

Marge throws her arms in the air and does a grapevine

into a jazz square. She is panting so hard she reminds me of Max, my dachshund, when he sits on my porch in the summertime. Her eyes are wild, and I'm pretty sure she's foaming at the mouth.

MARGE

OMG YOU NEED TO SING RIGHT NOW!!! GET ON
THAT STAGE!!!

Duke sneaks up to me, trembling.

DUKE

I don't know what happened. I was doing my thing,
and all of a sudden Marge started flipping out.
Someone must have told her I was in <u>Phantom</u> and
now she wants me to <u>sing</u> to her.

ME

Well, then sing to her.

DUKE

I don't want to, Henry.

I glance back at Marge, who is playing with a feather boa and grinding her hips.

ME

I'm not sure you have a choice.

Marge gets up on a tiny stage with the DJ and grabs a microphone.

MARGE

Testing, testing, one, two, three . . . la la la la la la la.
Thank you! Ladies and gentlemen, as you know, it's
my Sweet Sixteen, and tonight we have been
graced with a member of the Broadway cast of <u>The
Phantom of the Opera.</u>

Marge points at Duke. People applaud.

MARGE (cont.)

His name is Marcello, and for my birthday, I would
like him to sing me a song from the show, which
happens to be one of my favorites. Not my <u>favorite</u>
favorite, which is <u>Les Miz,</u> and not my second
favorite, <u>Ragtime.</u> 'Wheels of a Dream,' byotches!
It's not my third favorite either, but, well, it's
definitely Top Five. No, Top Ten. Anyway . . . without
further ado, I bring you . . . Marcello!

Duke looks to me for help. I shrug and start to laugh. This is so ridiculous.

He crawls to the stage as though he's about to be executed, and takes the microphone from Marge, who squeals.

DUKE

Uh, thank you.

There's no accompaniment, so everyone simply waits for Duke to begin. What seems like an eternity goes by before he presses his lips to the mic.

DUKE

I would <u>love</u> to sing for you, Marge, but since it's your Sweet Sixteen, the song should truly be a special one. I'm only in the chorus of <u>Phantom</u>; however, the Phantom himself is here with us tonight. (He points to me.) Give it up for my good friend, Don Carlos!

If there weren't over a hundred people staring at us, I would leap across the room and tackle Duke.

DUKE

Don't be shy, Don Carlos. Come on up.

Nigel pushes me forward and I give the crowd a fake smile. When I reach the stage, Duke passes me the microphone.

MARGE

Aren't you a little young to be the Phantom?

DUKE

Nah, you should see him with the mask on!

How can I get out of this? I could drop the mic and run, but Duke has the keys, and I'd have to wait for the valet to bring the car around—by that time Marge (or her parents) will have clobbered me to death.

MARGE

Well, sing to me already! Somebody SING to me!
It's my effing <u>birthday</u>!

Here goes nothing. I start with the first few words of "The Music of the Night." Even though the movie version sucked, I'm glad I saw it. I have a decent-enough voice. Although I forget a few of the words, I think Marge will be happy.

Toward the end (I sort of rushed through the middle,

let's be honest) I look over at Marge and she's crying.
Could I possibly be that . . . good? When I finish, her tears
are flowing pretty freely.

ME

Don't cry, Marge.

MARGE

IT'S MY PARTY AND I'LL CRY IF I WANT TO! You're
an AWFUL singer! (She turns to her mother.) What
has the state of musical theater come to?

DUKE

Actually, he's only the Phantom <u>understudy.</u>

ME

Let's go.

I pull Duke off the stage with me, grab Nigel, and dash
toward the exit.

We drive home in silence. Until:

ME

I can't believe that actually happened.

NIGEL

Well, I thought you were stellar. I wanted an encore.

ME

Bite me.

I turn to Duke.

ME (cont.)

You're a dead man, Duke. A dead man.

DUKE

If I gotta go, I gotta go. But man, was that shit funny.

12

GARRETT

"Tell us all about school!" my mother says at dinner. Since the move, we haven't eaten together often because of Dad's teaching schedule. Wednesday nights he's free, though, and we try to do something as a family. Usually this means ordering in (Mom isn't much of a cook), but tonight she's made her signature dish: spaghetti.

"Eat up, guys, or it'll go cold!" She pours more sauce onto my plate. "Isn't this delicious? It's my favorite recipe."

I want to say that boiling water and heating up a can of

Four Brothers doesn't qualify as a recipe, but I don't because, really, where will that get me?

"I tried this new pasta," Mom says, "and it's green! You probably can't tell because of the sauce, but it is. Green pasta. What will they think of next? It's made from spinach, I think. Organic spinach. Which is really healthy for you, honey"—she turns to my dad—"because of your high cholesterol."

"My cholesterol is just fine," he says, swallowing.

"That's not what Dr. Miller told you. Dr. Miller said that your cholesterol was through the roof! Can you imagine? Now, eat up." She wipes Dad's chin with her napkin. "You had a little sauce on you," she says, kissing him. Then she turns her attention back to me. "We're still waiting, Garrett—*how* is *school*?"

"It's fine," I say.

"What are your favorite classes?" Dad asks.

I think for a second. "I guess AP Lit and, I don't know, my creative writing elective."

"You always were such a wonderful writer," Mom says. "I've saved all the birthday cards you gave me, you know. Your words are like miniature poems. You've got a gift, dear. A gift. Don't let it go to waste."

I can't remember ever writing anything to my mother

other than *Happy Birthday, Mom. Love, Garrett,* but I don't correct her. "Uh, thanks."

"Any friends?" Dad asks.

"There are these girls. London, Jessica, and Jyllian. They're . . . nice." If the J Squad ever heard me describe them as *nice,* I think they would officially cut me off.

"That's great, sweetie," Dad says. "Any boys?"

My father has never liked any of my past boyfriends except for Ben, who he didn't *like* so much as *tolerate.* Not because they were bad guys—he's just leery of any teenagers with testosterone.

I wonder what Dad would think of my current actions: getting Henry to fall in love with me so I can dump him on television to teach him a lesson. I doubt he'd be very proud. Before I can answer, my mother says, "Oh no, honey. Garrett has sworn off men. Forever."

Dad raises an eyebrow. "Forever?"

"Just until college," I say.

He continues staring at me. "Good for you, sweetie. That's an excellent idea. Focus on your grades and applying to schools. Have you thought about where you want to go?"

I remember my conversation with Henry in his room. Why is the question from adults always *Have you thought* about *where you want to go?* and not *Have you thought about what you want to be? Who you want to be?*

"Not really," I say. "A little."

"You should," Dad says. "I can put you in touch with the Columbia admissions person for Long Island if you have any questions. Or the woman from U Chicago."

"Sure," I say. "That sounds fine."

"Oh, before I forget," Mom says, "we were invited to a party this weekend. A welcome-to-the-neighborhood kind of thing. One of the women who lives down the street invited me this afternoon. I *wanted* to say that we've been here for over a month already! Where was this party when we first arrived? But I didn't want to be rude, you know? Better late than never, I suppose."

"Sounds good," Dad says, leaning in and giving her a kiss. I think about when Henry kissed me this afternoon. "It'll be fun, I bet."

My parents have known each other since they were my age. They met in high school and started dating their junior year. They went to separate colleges but stayed together (aside from a six-month breakup that neither of them will speak about). They are totally and completely in love. I can't decide whether this makes me sick or insanely jealous.

I put down my fork. "May I be excused? I have a lot of homework."

"Sure, honey," Dad says. "Get to it!"

I leave the table and go upstairs, letting them have a few moments alone.

In my room, I sit down at my computer and check my e-mail. Nothing. I pick up my phone and dial Amy's number. It goes straight to voice mail. I don't leave a message. Why hasn't she returned any of my calls? This is getting ridiculous already.

I'm about to put my phone down when it buzzes. One new text message. From London.

Saw u with Henry @ lunch today. Good 4 u.

I write back:

All in a day's work.

Then she writes:

When's ur next date?

Good question. So far, I think I've played everything perfectly. Aside from getting the job at the cinema, all of my encounters with Henry have been initiated by him (even though they were manipulated by me). I haven't chased after him; I've let him take the lead. He was the one who started saying hello to me at school. Who invited me to watch *Annie Hall*. Who asked me to have lunch with him. Maybe now it's time to up the ante.

I open my Gmail account. I need to send something short and to the point. Flirty and intriguing rather than pushy and irritating. An e-mail that, when he opens it, will make him respond immediately.

To: henry.arlington@gmail.com
Subject: When are you…

Going to take me out on an actual date? Courtyard benches are nice and all, but sometimes a girl likes a good old-fashioned restaurant.

—G

I click Send and stare at my computer, waiting for a little (1) to appear next to the Inbox on the left side of the screen. I open my iTunes library and search for Adele. At least I can have some music while I wait.

I get through the first two songs on her album and am halfway through the third when a reply comes. I click it open.

Henry Arlington to me

You + Me = Friday. After school.

That's all it says. Five words, but I'm in. I close my eyes and lean back in my chair. *Good work, Garrett.* Then I reply to London's last text:

Friday

A few seconds later, she writes:

Lavish. See u tmrw!

I wonder where Henry will be taking me. I know it doesn't really matter what we do—it's the fact that we're going out that counts—but still. Were this an actual relationship, I'd be smitten with how adorable he's being (buying me a cookie?! Flirting via e-mail?!), but since it's *not* an actual relationship, any smitten-ness would be inappropriate on my part. Completely inappropriate.

I do my homework and get ready for bed. I watch TV and paint my nails. I go into iPhoto on my MacBook and find pictures from my seventeenth birthday; I drag all the ones with Ben in them to the trash except for a photo of me, him, and Amy. I'm still feeling restless. I begin unpacking some of the boxes from the move I've hidden underneath my bed. Lots and lots of books. My copy of Aimee Mann's *The Forgotten Arm*, the one I thought I'd lost. I still cannot stop thinking about Friday. What am I going to wear?

I'm searching through my closet—I have way too many sweaters—when I pause for a moment. It feels like I'm getting ready for a date, only this is *not* a real date. This is part of a game, a mission. I am going out with Henry because it's the next step in my plan to break his heart.

Only I can no longer think about Henry without remembering the way he kissed me, and what it felt like to be held by him and talk about life and love. I've never had such a frank, open conversation with anyone—not even Ben. I want to be happy that I found someone at my new school I truly connect with, but I can't because I'm not supposed to like Henry. I am supposed to destroy him.

But if I like Henry, actually *like* him, then I'm going against everything I said I wanted, mainly not putting my feelings at the mercy of some "high school boy," as London would put it.

Despite my confusion, one realization has emerged: this thing with Henry is complicated.

HENRY

INT.—MY BEDROOM, THURSDAY AFTERNOON

DUKE

Okay, how about this: we dress up in big chicken
costumes, like we work at KFC or something, we
have buckets full of fried chicken, and when
Destiny comes out we throw chicken everywhere!

NIGEL

No.

ME

No. And that's a waste of chicken.

DUKE

Okay, how about <u>this:</u> we dress up like pirates, with eye patches and a lot of gold chains, and Nigel, you can have a peg leg, and we talk in ridiculous accents and steal people's money.

NIGEL

I like the gold chains part. And the peg leg.

ME

You would.

NIGEL

But I feel like pirates are so 2003. We need something very <u>now.</u> Something that's never been done before.

DUKE

Remember when we put food coloring in everyone's water glasses at that Sweet Sixteen out in Montauk? We could do that again.

NIGEL

No. We can't repeat any old pranks. MTV is going

to be there! This is huge. Whatever we do has to

be . . . epic. It has to go down in history.

ME

I hardly think some random prank at a Sweet

Sixteen will go down in history.

DUKE

You know what'll go down in history?

NIGEL

(to me)

Henry, if we just ignore him, maybe he'll disappear.

ME

My brain hurts. I need a break.

I fall down on my bed and pretend to be asleep. Nigel is
sitting in the chair at my computer, and Duke has sunk
into the beanbag chair next to my closet.

ME

Put on some music.

NIGEL

What do you wanna listen to? There's this new
song I like called "Everyone at School Saw You
Having Lunch with Garrett Yesterday."

I open my eyes.

ME

Never heard of it.

DUKE

Henry, dude. Seriously. Lunch in the courtyard?
What were you thinking?

ME

It was just lunch.

I don't mention the fact that I'm taking Garrett on an actual date tomorrow night.

ME (cont.)

It's not a big deal.

NIGEL

Yes it is. Nothing is ever just lunch. Next thing we
know you'll be holding hands in the hallway or

something else absolutely revolting. You have to
stop this before it's too late.

ME

Why don't you guys just chill out and mind your
own business?

DUKE

You <u>are</u> our business!

NIGEL

You're our best friend, Henry, and this girl is no
good for you. No good.

ME

You don't even know her.

NIGEL

Neither do you! And you already hooked up with
her . . . what else is there to do?

I should tell them that originally, back at the Sweet
Sixteen in August, we didn't hook up. That I lied to them.
That I let them *think* we hooked up because I didn't know
what else to say. But I don't. I'd rather have them think
I'm a coward than a liar.

ME

You know, some guys actually <u>like</u> hooking up with
the same girl more than once.

Duke and Nigel wince as though I've said something incredibly offensive.

NIGEL

Oh, Henry. What's happened to you?

INT.–EAST SHORE HIGH SCHOOL, FRIDAY
MORNING

Today is the big day. I'm taking Garrett somewhere I
know she will love. I look sharp (I always do, but today especially) and I've written her a note saying to meet me after school in the student parking lot.

I leave Garrett's locker, and I'm walking down the senior hallway when someone taps my shoulder.

LONDON

Henry.

ME

Uh, hey.

Here's the deal with London: she's hot, scary, and I lost my virginity to her. It happened about two years ago. I was still a total wreck from my mom having left. London's mom isn't in the picture either—we sort of bonded over that. And she was sweet. After, though, she wanted to be my girlfriend and I wasn't ready for that kind of commitment. I broke it off. Then she turned into this hard-core biddy and became insanely popular and created the J Squad. We haven't had an actual conversation since.

I feel bad about what happened with London, and I still think about it sometimes. Realizing I suck at relationships is one of the reasons I started crashing Sweet Sixteens. It's clear to me that I hurt her, that I didn't handle things well, but I didn't know any better. And besides, that was years ago. I'm sure she's over it by now.

ME (cont.)

How are you? I'm surprised to see you alone. You usually travel in a pack.

LONDON

Let's not bother with small talk. We're past that. And you're not very funny.

ME

Okay . . .

LONDON

I just wanted to say that I saw you.

ME

Saw me what?

She motions to Garrett's locker.

ME

I was just—

LONDON

Do you like her?

ME

Garrett?

LONDON

Of course. Do you? Like her?

I'm silent.

LONDON (cont.)

Well?

ME

Why does it matter to you?

LONDON

(scowling)

If that's how you want to play this, Henry, then fine.

But I'm on to you.

She stomps away, and I am incredibly confused by what just happened. Why are girls so crazy?

Later, I'm waiting in Garrett's driveway when there's a tap on my car window. It's Garrett. I open the door and let her inside; Ryan Adams's album *Easy Tiger* is playing on my stereo. I am nervous but happy.

"Hey," she says.

"Hey."

"How was your day?"

"It was good," I tell her. "Better now that you're here."

She laughs, and I laugh too. Who is this person talking? *Better now that you're here?* I can't believe I just said those words, let alone *meant* them.

Garrett is wearing a simple black dress. She looks incredible. Something makes me want to take her in my arms and kiss her.

I do.

Then she looks at me in a way I don't think anyone has ever really looked at me before.

"So, are you ready for tonight?" I ask.

"Yeah," she says. "Where are we going? This is such a mystery!"

"What would you say if I told you I was taking you somewhere I can guarantee you've never been?"

She smiles. "I would say *let's go.*"

"This is so cool," Garrett says as we pull into the parking lot and find a spot. I've taken her to one—and my favorite—of the only drive-in movie theaters on Long Island. They're basically extinct, save a few classics that refuse to shut down. Most of the time they play old romantic comedies or horror flicks. Tonight? They're playing *Night of the Living Dead.*

"I hope this is okay," I tell her. "I didn't know if you liked scary movies, but I thought I'd take a chance."

She messes up my hair with her fingers. "It's great."

"Are you sure? I've never, um, you know. Been on a *date*

before. Not, like, a real one, anyway. Do you wanna go someplace fancy for dinner instead?"

"I have simple tastes, Henry. Give me a movie and some popcorn and I'm good to go."

"My kind of girl," I say, relieved. "I'll be right back."

I buy us popcorn, soda, and some Swedish Fish; when I get back, the movie is about to start.

"I asked for champagne but all they had was Diet Coke."

"What drive-in movie theater doesn't serve champagne to minors?" Garrett asks. "Who do they think they are?"

"I know, right? I'll have to file a complaint with the manager."

"If he's anything like Roger, it's probably not worth your time."

"I don't think *anyone* is like Roger," I say. My car is warm and the popcorn is incredibly buttery. Garrett takes a handful and licks her fingers clean.

"What are you looking at?" she asks.

"You."

"Why?"

"I'm just thinking about all the things I'd change about your face."

"What?" She slaps me on the arm—playfully. "Henry!"

"I'm kidding," I say. "You know you're beautiful."

"I'm already out with you, Henry. You don't have to lie."

"You do know how beautiful you are, right? I mean, you're gorgeous."

She blushes. "Okay, okay, Casanova. How about we focus on the movie, huh?"

Night of the Living Dead is gross. Garrett rests her head on my shoulder the entire time. Occasionally, she'll scream and her hand will touch my leg or mine will touch hers and I swear to God it's electric. Our connection isn't just physical, either. I anticipate her every reaction: which parts of the movie she'll laugh at because she'll think they're stupid, which parts she'll close her eyes during because they're too grotesque, which parts she'll be totally consumed by. And I know how she's going to respond because it's the *exact same way* I do.

There's a moment when one of the characters discovers that her daughter has been turned into one of the living dead; even though there's nothing sexy or romantic or anything remotely like that about this particular scene, I watch Garrett watching the movie, feel her holding my hand, and look up at the roof of my car. I pretend I can see right through the padding and the metal into the night and whisper *Thank you.*

"Did you have a nice time?" I ask. The movie is over and we're about to say goodbye. I don't want the night to end, but it's late and, well, nothing lasts forever.

"I had a wonderful time," she says, resting her head on the window. The sky is so dark it looks black. My iPod is hooked up to my stereo and I'm playing Sinatra's "Fly Me to the Moon."

"Do you like this song?"

"Yeah," Garrett says. "Of course."

"Fly me to the moon, and let me play among the stars," I croon, turning my hand into a microphone and doing my best Sinatra impression.

Garret chimes in: "In other words, please be trueeee! In other words, I love you."

The song ends, and we both sit there. "You have a great voice," I say.

"You're sweet. But no, I don't. I'm like . . . a step away from tone-deaf."

She smiles, and I can't help myself: I kiss her. Softly at first, and then I search for her tongue with mine. Eventually we break for air, and she says, "Next time we go to the movies, we should get our popcorn with less butter." Then she kisses me again and says, "It's time for me to go."

"Not yet," I say. "Just a little longer."

"Sorry, kiddo, but I have a curfew. You don't want me to turn into a pumpkin, do you?"

I have never really understood why people call it *falling* in love but now, tonight, I do. Because when I drop Garrett off and watch her wave goodbye, I feel like I am furiously out of control and falling fast. But also I feel like I'm flying, like there is wind and air beneath me. I don't think you can fall and fly at the same time, though; I don't understand how it would work. It seems that eventually one will win out over the other, and I'm pretty sure it's much easier to crash than it is to soar.

14

GARRETT

"There's something different about you," my mother tells me. Henry and I have been spending every afternoon together for the past week, but I came home from school on my own today because the J Squad wants to have an early dinner at this Italian place called Baci.

"What do you mean?"

Mom is wearing a bandana and a magenta leotard. She just got back from the gym and is dripping with sweat. "Are you pregnant?"

"What? No."

"Are you sure?"

"Yes."

"Because I'm really too young to be a grandmother," she says, taking a bottle of water out of the fridge and downing it.

"You have nothing to worry about. I promise."

"Good. So what do you want for dinner? Turkey? Not like I cooked a turkey. I do have cold cuts, though. I could make you a sandwich."

"That's okay. I'm eating dinner with some friends from school."

"Those girls you've been talking about?" She looks at me as though I've been lying about the J Squad these past few weeks.

"Yes, Mother. *Those girls.* Don't look so surprised."

"I'm not. Or rather, I am a little bit, but I'm glad you're making friends. Friends who don't have penises. Can I meet them? Just to make sure they don't only exist in your head?"

"No."

"Why not?"

"Because you'll embarrass me. And these are *new* friends. I don't want to scare them away."

"You know," she says, taking off the bandana and

dabbing the back of her neck with it, "when I was in high school I had dozens of friends. *Millions.* I was friend central. No one thought I was embarrassing then!"

"Yeah, well, times change. What can I tell you. I've gotta get ready."

"Have you spoken to Amy recently?" she yells as I'm running up the stairs. "How's she doing?"

"Fine," I say, even though I have no idea if this is actually true.

"Tell her I say *yodelay hee hoo!* the next time you talk to her," Mom screeches.

Sure. And I'll tell her a whole lot more than that.

I almost forget how mad I am at Amy for dropping the ball on our friendship, because dinner with the J Squad is really "Fabulous" (Paul McCartney, 1999). I never realized how silly things can get with a few girls, some pasta, and a cute waiter.

"How come I've never seen you guys at any parties?" Devin, our waiter, asks us. When he'd mentioned that he went to Hofstra, we'd told him we were first-semester sophomores there.

"We don't really party," Jyllian says. "We mostly stay in and play with my Ouija board."

"Really?" he asks.

"We're trying to communicate with the ghost of my dead twin," London says. "She was trampled by a horse."

Devin looks really sad. "I'm so sorry."

"That's okay," London says casually. "She was fat. Can I have another Diet Coke?"

"Uh, sure."

"I love messing with waiters," she says once he's gone. "They're all so . . . gullible."

"You know what else are gullible? Fish," I say, pretending my hands are gills.

No one laughs.

"So I've narrowed down my dress options for Destiny's Sweet Sixteen," Jyllian says. The invitations came in the mail the other day—I was invited!—and according to the J Squad, figuring out what to wear is going to occupy pretty much the entire month of October.

"What color scheme are you going with?" Jessica asks, biting into a breadstick and slipping another one into her purse. "Rainbow?"

"Black," Jyllian says. "I want something classic and slutty, but not *slutty* slutty, you know? *Classy* slutty. Clutty. I want guys watching MTV to want me, not think I'm a whore."

"But you *are* a whore," London says. "No offense."

"None taken," Jyllian says, turning to me and shrugging. "I kind of am."

"I want to wear something lavish and purple," London says, "but not bright purple. Sort of a dull purple."

"Lavender?" Jessica asks.

"Absolutely not," London says, looking horrified. "Lavender is for freaks. That color is *so* rusty."

"Oh, right. Of course."

"What about you, Garrett?"

I haven't thought much about my dress yet, but I like things that are simple and elegant. And somewhat affordable. "I actually saw a dress at Anthropologie the other day that was really cute. It was teal, but not in a tacky way."

"OMG," Jessica says, "I know *exactly* which dress you're talking about. It would look *lavish* on you. You have to get it."

"I think I will."

Amy is (was—are we even friends anymore?) kind of tomboyish; she plays lacrosse and soccer, and her idea of dressing up is *not* wearing a pair of cleats. I can't even begin to imagine talking about Sweet Sixteens and dresses and shopping with her. While those things aren't my entire life, they are *part* of my life. It's nice to have girlfriends to share that with.

"So," London says while we're figuring out what to order for dessert, "what's the latest Henry update?"

"He's in my gym class, and this morning we were doing sit-ups, and I wasn't his partner but I was *next* to his partner, and I peeked over while he was doing them—he can do *so* many—and I'm not sure but, like, I *think* I saw his balls," Jyllian says without stopping to breathe.

London smacks her. "I wasn't talking to you. I was talking to Garrett."

Jyllian giggles. "Oh. Right." She leans forward and says, "If they *were* his balls, then they're *huge.*"

"That's enough," London says. "Really."

I can't help but laugh. One of the reasons I like the J Squad is because, well, they're outrageous. "Henry's good," I say. "Things are good."

"Details!" Jessica demands, taking a straw out of her purse and dropping it into her drink. "Juicy ones!"

I tell them about our "date" to the drive-in. What I *don't* tell them is how much we've spoken since then—every night—and how oddly special the time we spend together is. When I agreed to the J Squad's bet, I never imagined Henry would turn into someone I could actually see myself dating. Of course, there's my personal mantra: *I don't want a boyfriend.* Only, Henry makes me wonder if said mantra is actually true.

"I cannot believe Henry Arlington took you on a *date*," Jyllian says. "He's never done that. For anyone. And I mean *anyone*." She shoots London a sideways glance. "Not even you."

Not even you? What does that mean? I stare at London for a hint, but she doesn't provide one.

"What's he like?" Jessica asks, sighing. "I mean, what's he *really* like? When you're alone together."

I don't want to reveal too much, but I also want them to know how far along I am in this "LoveGame" (Lady Gaga, 2008). "He's very sweet," I tell them, "and he really likes movies. He's very smart about film in general."

"More!" Jessica says. "Tell us more!"

I notice that London is completely silent.

Finally, she says: "I heard he crashed a Sweet Sixteen in Carle Place the other night."

He did?

"Are you sure?" I ask.

"I'm sure," she says, nodding. "He can't like you that much if he's still crashing parties, Garrett."

Her tone implies that I have failed, somehow. It frustrates me. If Henry's still crashing Sweet Sixteens, I've got my work cut out for me.

"I wonder if he hooked up with anyone," Jessica says. "That would be so . . . rusty."

I can't help but wonder the very same thing. I thought we connected during our date. But maybe it wasn't enough. Maybe I need to do more.

"Did you guys decide on a dessert?" Devin asks, seemingly coming out of nowhere.

"Yes," Jyllian says, squishing her boobs together with her arms. "We'll have the tiramisu for two for four."

"Coming right up!"

"And a cappuccino," London calls after him.

"And another one," Jessica says.

"Make that three," I say. Then I look at Jyllian. "Do you want one?"

She shakes her head. "Oh, no thanks. My parents don't believe in cappuccino."

"What?"

"They think it's the devil's drink."

"Back to you," says London, reapplying lip gloss with her pinky. "It sounds like you really like him. Like, *really* like him."

I need to steer this conversation away from dangerous territory. "I have no desire to date Henry. I just want to win."

London looks at me skeptically. "Are you sure?"

My hands start shaking and I hide them under the table. "Absolutely."

"Well, whatever you do," she says, smacking her lips together and staring at me with smoldering eyes, "don't fall in love with him."

I try to mirror her intensity, but instead of coming off *smoldering*, I come off *cross-eyed*.

"Did your contacts dry up?" Jyllian asks. "I have re-wetting drops in my bag."

"I'm fine."

"Because you look a little wonky . . ."

"Garrett *said* she was fine," London says sharply. She continues to stare at me, even once the cappuccinos arrive and the tiramisu disappears and we pay the bill. She only breaks her gaze when it's time to leave.

"So how was dinner?" Henry asks me later that night on the phone. It's incredible, really—the way he pays attention to everything I say.

"Fine," I say. "We talked a lot about Destiny's Sweet Sixteen. They're all really excited."

"I'm sure." I can hear the laughter in his voice. God knows what he thinks of the J Squad. Probably that they're nasty and why the hell am I friends with them anyway? I want to ask whether he's hooked up with any of them, but I can't tell if Henry is someone who likes to talk about that kind of stuff or not. I assume *not*. He hasn't asked me about any of my past relationships (not that I want him to—awkward), but it does strike me as odd that we're skirting around the fact that *I know* he has a reputation as a total player. I'm dying to know why he told people that we hooked up, and why he's still crashing parties, but I keep my mouth shut.

"Are *you* excited?" he asks.

"I guess. I've never been to anything that's been filmed for TV before."

"I was an extra once," he says.

"Really?"

"Not on purpose or anything. I was at this amusement park a few years ago and they were filming that awful movie with Hugh Grant and Drew Barrymore, where he's some, like, aging pop star."

"*Music and Lyrics*?"

"That's it. Anyway, you see my face for all of five seconds."

"Wow," I say. "I had no idea I was talking to a movie star."

"Oh yeah, baby. You know it."

There's a bit of silence after he calls me baby, even though I know he meant it casually.

"Well," I say, "*you* must be pretty excited for Destiny's big bash."

"Oh?"

"Seeing as how you love Sweet Sixteens and all."

He laughs.

"It's true!"

"I'm actually not," he says. "That excited."

"Why not?"

"I'd rather just hang out with you."

More silence. Honesty. I am about to say *We could just skip it and watch a movie,* but the entire point of this charade is to show up with Henry as his date. I know that if I *do,* he'll get his feelings hurt, and if I *don't,* the J Squad will make my life miserable. Either way, this has become a lose-lose situation.

I go back and forth about how to respond until I remember the rumor about us hooking up and why I started on this quest in the first place.

"We could go together," I suggest. "You could show me what a Sweet Sixteen is like through Henry Arlington's eyes. If you want."

"I'd love to," he says. Judging from how quickly he answers, I know he means it. "I would love to go with you."

This makes me feel a bunch of things at once: happiness (at getting one step closer to completing the J Squad's plan), sadness (at getting one step closer to screwing

Henry over), and general confusion about how to move forward.

"Okay then," I say. "It's settled."

We continue talking about anything and everything. There is no filter with Henry. We talk about movies and music and art and TV and Duke and Nigel and the J Squad and college basketball (he's a Duke fan). Before I know it, it's practically three a.m. We've been on the phone for nearly four hours.

"We've been talking for a long time," I say.

"I know. I don't think I've ever had a conversation with anyone that lasted longer than five minutes."

I've had longer conversations than that, sure, but never like this. Not even with Ben. I don't say anything. I am thinking about what—if anything, and surely the ease at which we can communicate is *something*—this means.

"You know what's crazy?" he asks.

"No. What?"

He takes a breath that is so deep I can hear it. "I could keep talking to you. Forever."

I'm not heartless, you know. When I hear him say this, everything inside me screams *Tell him about the bet you made with the J Squad!* I don't, though. If I tell him, he will stop talking to me; I'll lose the bet and then I will be left with no one. With nothing. And I do like talking to Henry.

A lot, actually. But I also like hanging out with the J Squad.

I'm not sure what to do. I need more time to think.

"I'm tired," I say. "I should probably go."

"Okay," he says, sounding slightly disappointed. "See you tomorrow?"

"Mm-hmm. G'night."

I hang up the phone and wonder if I'm a terrible, horrible person or if, unwittingly, the game I have been playing is in fact playing me.

15

HENRY

In 2002, the American Film Institute (AFI) published a list of the one hundred greatest love stories on film. I don't particularly believe in lists like this one (what qualifies the AFI to decide the "best" movies in any genre?), but Roger thought it would be a good gimmick for the cinema, so starting tonight we're showing the Top Ten films on the AFI's list, one per night.

ROGER
It'll be good for couples. Y'know. Romantic and shit.

When I ask Garrett to see all ten movies with me, I assume she will say no. It'll require some rearranging of our work schedules, and I ask her mostly as a joke anyway, but she says yes without hesitation.

I am pleasantly surprised.

It's been a long time since I've been to Huntington as a moviegoer. I've traded in my uniform for a light blue V-neck sweater and a pair of jeans. "This is me going to pick up a girl," I say out loud, dabbing on some cologne and heading out the door.

Now that I've broken the No Dating seal by taking Garrett to *Night of the Living Dead*, there's nothing else to do but go full-steam ahead. To drive at a reckless speed and see what will happen and hope I don't get hurt.

INT.–HUNTINGTON CINEMAS

(It Takes) Ten Movies to Fall in Love

10. <u>City Lights</u>, 1931

Monday Night

Garrett and I watch this movie in one of the smaller theaters. She's wearing a dress that shows off her bare shoulders and she smells like honey. *City Lights* is a silent Charlie Chaplin movie in which he plays his slapstick tramp character, but this particular film happens to be pretty heartfelt. The tramp falls in love with a blind flower seller, who mistakes him for a millionaire, and Chaplin tries to raise money to pay for surgery that will restore the girl's eyesight.

I'm a huge Chaplin fan, and the movie doesn't disappoint. I've seen it before, but I forgot how touching the ending is, when Chaplin is released from prison (he's mistakenly arrested for stealing money) and encounters the flower girl months after her surgery, and she can see. Or maybe *forgot* is the wrong word. Maybe I never realized how touching the ending is in the first place.

9. Love Story, 1970

Tuesday Night

This movie is about a guy named Oliver whose family is all Harvard grads and are generally pretty stuck-up. He meets a spunky girl named Jenny who goes to Radcliffe and they fall in love. They graduate from college and decide to get married. Oliver goes to Harvard Law School, and when Jenny wants to have children, it becomes clear (to Oliver, at least) that she has cancer.

I'm not wild about the premise. I think it's pretty sappy (she dies, and Oliver reunites with his father, who'd shunned him), and I don't think there's anything too inventive about the storytelling.

"Do you like this?" I whisper to Garrett about halfway through.

"No. I want more popcorn."

"I like the way you think."

8. <u>It's a Wonderful Life</u>, 1946

Wednesday Night

A guy about to commit suicide is visited by his guardian angel, who helps him appreciate life by showing him what the world would be like if he'd never been in it. Sort of cheesy, but the good kind of cheese (e.g., Brie).

"Was that screenplay written by a man?" Garrett asks once it's over. We're outside the theater, walking to my car.

"I have no idea. Maybe?"

"I bet it was," she says, shaking her head. "Why is it

that if George hadn't existed, Mary would be some old spinster librarian? She was cute. Are you seriously going to tell me she couldn't have found another guy? I don't buy it. It's totally misogynistic."

"I think you're reading into it too much," I tell her. She seems really enraged; I'm totally turned on by the fact that she has such a strong reaction to the film.

I kiss her.

"You taste good," I say. "Like M&M's." When I look at her, I feel so much. "Are we crazy?"

"Maybe. I don't know. Kiss me again," she says, and it almost sounds like she's begging for it.

7. Doctor Zhivago, 1965

Thursday Night

This movie is hard to follow. I think it's all the Russian names. It's based on a book about this guy, Dr. Zhivago. It's set against the Russian Revolution of 1917 (and, I think, another war that follows). A lot of the film is about how Zhivago's ideals and dreams as a young man are ripped apart by the violence in his country. He is torn between the love of his life (Lara) and his wife (Tonya).

I can definitely relate to the guy-with-two-ladies aspect,

but I don't particularly like movies with characters who "tell the story" in flashbacks, and neither does Garrett. The movie is also way too long. There is something endearing about it, though.

"The score was beautiful," Garrett says on the way home. "Isn't it interesting how music can really make or break a film?"

"What do you mean?"

"Just that, you know, the actors don't hear the music when they're performing. It's added in afterwards. Yet it's so important. It totally sets the tone. I can't imagine a movie without music."

I agree. "That'd be a pretty cool job, huh?"

"What?"

"Picking the songs that get played in movies. Figuring out exactly where they go. Working with the composer on the score. That kind of thing."

I watch her; I can tell she's seriously contemplating this. "Yeah," she says, "it would."

I ask her to come back to my house, but she declines. "We're still on for tomorrow, right?"

"We are," I say.

She kisses me so softly I can barely feel her lips on mine. I wrap my arms around her. *Don't stop,* I think. *I'm wild about you. Don't stop.*

Eventually, she stops, opening the car door and stepping outside. "Good night, Henry," she says.

Later that night, I check my phone. Four voice mails. Two from Duke, two from Nigel, wondering where the hell I am, and why I haven't returned any of their calls. I debate calling them back (I know it's rude not to, and I'm only delaying the inevitable), but there's really only one person I want to talk to.

Even though I just saw her, I dial up Garrett. We talk about things like whether Dr. Zhivago was actually a doctor and if we could eat anything *right now* what would it be and what it means in the Killers' "Human" when Brandon Flowers sings the line "Are we human or are we dancer?" even though it doesn't really matter because we both love the song so much.

I fall asleep with the phone on my pillow. I know this because I wake up in the middle of the night and feel it there, and I wish so hard that it were Garrett resting next to me.

6. The Way We Were, 1973

Friday Night

"You're not sick of me yet?" I ask jokingly. As soon as the words are formed, though, I realize it's not really a joke. I'm nervous. Is she tired of me? Am I boring her?

"Shut up, Henry," she tells me, turning on the radio in my car. "And drive. I don't want to miss the movie. I love this one."

Barbra Streisand plays an intense political activist who marries Robert Redford even though they don't have all that much in common. They have a baby, and once they, you know, realize they don't have all that much in common, get a divorce. Years later, they meet in New York. Redford has a new gal and seems happy; Streisand is also shacking up with another dude. Basically, Redford realizes that no one has ever challenged him like Streisand did, and even though he's middle-of-the-road happy, he'll never have everything without her. At least, that's how I interpret it.

There's something to be said, I think, for the past remaining in the past. So many people try holding on to things that simply aren't working: jobs, friendships, relationships. Maybe certain things only exist in a certain time, though. Maybe things aren't meant to last forever. And that doesn't mean they didn't change our lives. Garrett and I sit and watch the credits and I wonder how long this whole thing between us is going to last, and what I will be left with once it's over.

5. <u>An Affair to Remember</u>, 1957

Saturday Night

Garrett and I are working tonight, so we skip this one. I've already seen it anyway. Missed connections, misunderstandings, pride, injury, Cary Grant, and true love. It's a pretty good film, but after five days of melodrama I'm in need of a rest.

After our shift, Garrett comes over to my house. She hasn't met my father yet; tonight he's already retreated to his room when we come home.

"He works a lot," I say casually, as if that explains his behavior.

Upstairs, we make out for a while and listen to James Morrison's album *Songs for You, Truths for Me.*

"He must really miss your mom," Garrett says, still in her work clothes. I run my hands up and down her back, pressing her body to mine. I feel her shiver.

"He does," I say. "A lot."

I have never spoken about my mother to anyone, except for Duke and Nigel. Even then, I never revealed how much my father still longs for her.

"How did she die? If you don't mind me asking."

I've been waiting for this question. It's the moment of truth. It would be so easy to lie and make something up. *Oh, cancer. You know how it is.* But I look at Garrett, I feel her against me, and I know I cannot lie anymore. Not to her.

"I have to tell you something," I say. "My mother isn't dead."

She pulls back a little. "She's not?"

"No. At least, I don't think so. She left when I was twelve and I haven't heard from her since. I have no idea where she is or what she's doing. I told you she was dead because, well, basically she is. To me. She's dead to me."

Garrett slips her arms around my waist and hugs me. I feel a light wetness on my skin; I can't tell if it's her kisses or her tears.

"Henry," she says quietly. "I don't know what to say."

"It's okay," I tell her.

But it's not okay, and we both know it. I try to cry and mourn the loss of my mother, but I can't. Nothing escapes. So I hold still and let Garrett feel the things I cannot seem to feel, and hope that someday I will be able to grieve like she can.

4. <u>Roman Holiday,</u> 1953

Sunday Afternoon

Trouble arrives around eleven a.m. in the form of Duke and Nigel, who pull up to my house just as I'm about to leave.

They run toward me and bang on the window of my Jeep.

ME

Uh, hey, guys.

DUKE

Where ya goin', Henry?

ME

Work.

NIGEL

We've been calling you all weekend.

ME

I know, I know. I'm sorry. I've just been crazy busy.

DUKE

Doing what?

ME

Stuff . . . with my dad.

They look at me as if I'm going to elaborate. But since I'm lying, I figure brief is best.

NIGEL

You're <u>always</u> busy these days. What gives? Didn't
you have fun the other night, Phantom?

ME

No. A little. I don't know.

DUKE

You don't have to keep us in the dark, dude. Tell us
what's going on.

NIGEL

We're worried about you, Henry.

I should just tell them things are getting serious with me and Garrett, but all I can think about is how much shit they'll give me for ditching them and getting involved in something, well, serious. For abandoning the Crasher Code and keeping it from them.

ME

Look, I'm gonna be late. I'll text you guys later.

I know they deserve a friend who can open up and let them in. Deep down, I *want* to be that person. But until I can, I'd rather put the inevitable confrontation off for as long as possible.

Our shift doesn't start until later, so Garrett and I watch what I'll call one of the best romantic comedies I have ever seen. Audrey Hepburn plays a princess who is pretty overloaded; she pretends to be a commoner and wanders around Rome with the help of Gregory Peck's character, a reporter who realizes her identity but keeps quiet in the hopes of scoring an exclusive story and some pictures of her to sell for a lot of money.

Peck ultimately winds up doing the right thing, but he and Audrey don't get together in the end. It's not sad, though. You finish the film with a smile on your face, wondering what might have been between the two of them but glad they got the chance to meet.

"Are you okay?" Garrett asks during our break. We're standing outside, drinking fountain sodas and leaning against the brick wall of the cinema.

"Sure. Well, I don't know. I think Nigel and Duke are mad at me."

"For what?"

"Spending time with you," I say.

"Are you upset?"

"I mean, sort of. Yeah. What can I do, though? I'm not going to stop seeing you, which is what they want."

"It doesn't have to be all or nothing," Garrett tells me. "I'm sure they want you to be happy."

I shake my head. "It's hard to explain. They've been my friends since forever. I wouldn't have made it this far without them. But it's complicated. . . . They wouldn't approve of you and me."

"Why not?" Garrett asks.

I shrug. "They just wouldn't."

There's a thoughtful expression on her face. "Despite what you may think, I know a thing or two about complicated friendships." She touches my shoulder and says, "You know, we haven't really spoken about last night."

"What's there to talk about?"

"Your mom . . ."

"There's not much else to say." I'm not harsh, but my tone is definitely *I don't want to have this particular conversation right now.* Which is true. Being emotional at night when you're in bed with someone is one thing; doing it in the daylight is something else entirely. I don't know if I'm ready for that.

"I think there's a lot to say."

"Garrett, can we talk about this later?" I ask. There is a hint of pleading in my voice, and she picks up on it.

"Okay. Later."

3. West Side Story, 1961

Monday Night

"There's nothing better than star-crossed love," Garrett says emphatically. She's hooked up her iPod to my car stereo and is playing one of the songs from *West Side Story*, which we're on our way to see.

The song is called "One Hand, One Heart." It's basically about two people becoming one, and how the only thing that can separate them is death, and even death isn't enough to keep them apart forever.

"Isn't it romantic?" she asks, resting her hand on my knee.

I am still getting used to having a girl—the same girl—touch me day after day. My instinct is to push her away and say *Stay on your own side of the car,* but there is something comforting about Garrett's touch, about the ease and confidence with which she handles me, as if there is no doubt in her mind that I want her to touch me. What would it be like to be that kind of person?

"Nothing says romantic more than dying," I tease.

"Oh, you know what I mean."

And the funny thing is that, yes, I do.

2. <u>Gone with the Wind,</u> 1939

Tuesday Night

I could try to explain everything that happens in this movie, but I would fail miserably. It's nuts. The main character's name is Scarlett O'Hara, and she has a lot of husbands even though she only loves one man, who is married to someone else; eventually, she realizes she actually loves the man she is married to (her third husband), but it's too late. In the end, all she's left with is her home and her hope.

"I have no desire to end up like her," Garrett whispers. "One guy is enough for me, thanks."

"You won't," I assure her.

Me, on the other hand? I'm not so sure.

1. <u>Casablanca</u>, 1942

Wednesday Night

Clearly one of the best films ever. Humphrey Bogart sacrifices his love for Ingrid Bergman and does the "right thing," sending her off to America with her husband while a war rages in Europe.

Sucks.

"I wish he'd left with her in the end," Garrett says.

"He couldn't have. She would have hated him for it, ultimately."

She considers this. "Maybe. But maybe not. What if he made the wrong decision?"

"At least he made a decision. Didn't keep her in limbo."

"So making any decision at all is more important than making the right decision?"

"No, I'm not saying that. But what's right? There are no 'right' decisions in life. There are just decisions. And people make them. Then they deal with the consequences."

Garrett touches my chin with her hand. "You think a lot of things."

I laugh. "And that's bad?"

"No. It's wonderful. There's so much inside you. Every day I see you there is more and more."

I'm unsure where she's going with this.

She kisses my cheek. "It means you're human."

"Did you ever think I wasn't?"

"I had my doubts."

Ingrid Michaelson's "Be OK" is playing, and we listen to her wispy voice as I drive.

"So, is now 'later'?" Garrett asks.

"What do you mean?"

"You said you would tell me more about your mom later. You don't have to if you don't want to, but I'd really like to hear about her. And about you."

I pull into her driveway and turn off the engine. I sit silently for a few seconds before answering, "Why?"

"Because I want to know you, Henry."

I have never had anyone want to know me. I have never had anyone I *want* to want to know me. And here is this remarkable girl sitting next to me asking all the right questions. And I think: *So what if she leaves someday? Is that a good enough reason to shut her out? Would it be so wrong to let her in? Is she going to run away as soon as she realizes how incredibly fucked up I am? And so what if she does? Would I care?*

Yes. I would care.

"Okay," I tell her. "What do you want to know?"

"Everything," she says, reaching for my hand in the dark and finding it. "I want to know everything."

And so I tell her. What it was like to one day not have a mother anymore, to know that she was out there, somewhere, but that it was more important to her to live her life—however she's living it—than to be with me. How it felt to miss her every single day, clinging to the most insignificant things (the way she brushed her hair, the sound of her making breakfast every morning), until now, when the recollections I have of the woman who gave birth to me, who helped raise me for the first twelve years of my life, are like copies from a printer that has run out of ink.

"My dad boxed up all her pictures in our basement about a year after she left, once he realized she wasn't coming back. I used to go down there every day and look through them, hoping that if I closed my eyes and wished hard enough she would just appear." I try to laugh, but the sound gets caught in my throat. "One day, I stopped looking at them because they made me so angry, and so sad." Garrett squeezes my hand. "How can someone you love just leave you?"

Then it happens. Suddenly and surely and finally, I am crying. I don't know if it's for my mother or myself or both of us, but it doesn't really matter. The tears spill out and I can't stop them. Garrett whispers "Shh" in my ear, and "It's okay, I'm here," and I don't feel like a baby for crying in front of her, which kind of surprises me. I just feel like me.

Later, I lie awake in bed and ache for her. I wish she were next to me, her hand on my chest, her legs wrapped around mine. Because being with Garrett, well, it's the first time I haven't felt alone since my mother left. And the interesting thing about not being alone, the good thing, the revelation, is that it feels much better than being by yourself.

16

GARRETT

"On a scale of one to ten, ten being Rachel McAdams, nine being Rihanna, eight being Lindsay Lohan when she filmed *Mean Girls,* seven being Beyoncé, six being Kim Kardashian's ass, five being Kelly Clarkson, four being Jordin Sparks's thighs, three being the girl from the *Hairspray* movie remake, two being Raven-Symoné, and one being Rosie O'Donnell, how does this dress make me look?"

The J Squad and I are standing in the dressing room area of Betsey Johnson at the mall. London is trying on a strapless white gown with tiny flowers embroidered in blues and purples.

Jyllian squints and tells London to turn around. "Eleven?"

"*I* think you look like sunshine," says Jessica, who is trying on a pink dress and twirling in front of the mirror.

"Shut up," London says, smacking her. "G, what do you think?"

"You look cute," I say, "but like, *too* cute. Like you're thirteen or something."

"Ugh," London says. A few minutes later, she's back in her regular clothes. "Thanks for being honest," she tells me. "You're such a good friend."

"Of course."

"Jessica, are you getting that dress?" London asks.

Jessica stops twirling. "I don't think so. When I spin, you can't see my underwear."

London sighs. "All right. Let's go, then."

Jessica and Jyllian go to Bloomingdale's, while London and I go to Anthropologie. Luckily, they have the dress I like in my size.

"How does it look?" London asks, standing outside my changing room.

"Not sure yet," I say. There's a knock on the door. "I don't need anything else, thanks!"

"It's just me," London says.

I undo the lock and she slips inside. "Here." London zips the back. "Turn around."

The dress is gorgeous. I feel shiny and new. "What do you think?"

For a moment I wonder whether London's going to say something curt, which is sort of her way. "It's great," she says. "It's perfect for you."

"Thanks," I tell her, surprised by the compliment. "I'm glad you like it."

And I am. I'm glad that she is here with me and that she thinks the dress looks good on me, because her opinion is important. I try to forget about Henry, about all his kisses and the way he makes me laugh. I've had boyfriends before. Shopping and spending time with girlfriends—*this* is what I've been missing my entire life. I suddenly want to be in the J Squad so badly that it hurts.

London smiles at me. "You know, I'm really happy your family moved to Long Island."

Oh?

"You're just what we needed. Something to spice up senior year. I can't wait for Destiny's party to be over and for you to be an official member of the J Squad, you know?"

I want to say: *Why do we have to wait until after the party? You're the one who made up the rules. Can't you just break them?*

"Me too," I say.

London sighs dramatically. "Okay, dear. I'll be right across the hall if you need me. You can't be the *only* one who looks hot for all the cameras!"

I close the door behind her and look in the mirror. Really look. I am all sharp lines and dark hair. I try to picture myself stepping out of a limo and walking into Destiny's party with Henry by my side. *Henry.* I think about his mother leaving. I think about how hard it was for him to tell me that he was alone and sad, to tell me about his father crying (and Henry crying!) and what it felt like to grow up without anyone really standing by him, supporting him. My parents, despite their general craziness, have been the complete opposite. If anything, they care *too* much.

The longer I stare, the heavier my heart gets. There is one flaw in my plan with the J Squad that I'd never truly anticipated until it was staring me in the face: falling for Henry Arlington. Is it possible to stop in midair? To catch myself from landing splat on the pavement and breaking into a million pieces? Because no matter what happens, the one thing I *can't* foresee is a happy ending.

At home, I take out my guitar. The strumming relaxes me. I can smell my mother fixing dinner, and my dad is still at work "In the City" (The Eagles, 1979).

I've only been playing for a few minutes when my phone rings. I figure it's Jessica or Jyllian calling to gossip, or Henry, but when I look at the screen I'm so surprised I nearly fall off my chair.

I accept the incoming call and wait. I feel like I just swallowed a million packets of Pop Rocks.

"Hello?"

"Hi," I say.

"Garrett?"

That voice. It's him.

"Hi, Ben. How are you?"

"Good," he says casually, as though he didn't dump me the last time we spoke. As though there hasn't been radio silence between us. As though he didn't "Shut Up and Let Me Go" (The Ting Tings, 2008). "You?"

"Oh, you know. Fine."

"It's been a while, huh?"

That's the understatement of the century. Pop quiz. Should I:

A. Cry
B. Scream
C. Cry while screaming
D. Demand to know why he didn't return my texts or my calls
E. Tell him that I miss him
F. Read some of the poetry he wrote me last year and ask if all the times he compared me to a [insert flower type here] were lies
G. Tell him he's an asshole
H. Tell him I'll pay for him to fly halfway across the country and visit me
I. Tell him I'll never see him again, even if he does fly halfway across the country to visit me
J. Say random things in Spanish and hope he hangs up
K. Hang up
L. Tell him he has the wrong number
M. Ask if he remembers the time we hooked up on a blanket in my backyard when no one was home
N. Ask him if he remembers the time we hooked

up while my old golden retriever, Daisy, watched
us and barked

O. Read him some of the e-mails I wrote to him
that I never sent

P. Deny sending the ones I did send and claim
that someone hacked into my Gmail account

Q. Cry again, but harder this time and less intelligibly

R. Quote Shakespeare

S. Quote 50 Cent

T. Quote Taylor Swift

U. Sing him a song I wrote about how we're meant
to be together despite everything

V. Sing him a song I wrote about how much I hate
him and never want him back

W. A and J

X. M and S

Y. All of the above

Z. None of the above

I go with Z. "Yeah, it sure has been."

"It's good to hear your voice," he says.

"Is it?"

"Sure."

"Is that why you've called me so often?" So much for
playing it cool. I try picturing him in his bedroom. Is he at

his desk? On his bed? What is he wearing? I feel oddly numb. I would have thought that talking to Ben for the first time since we broke up would elicit some huge emotional response on my end, but it doesn't. I'm not even sure how much I really miss him.

Finally, I ask, "So, how's good old Mercer High?"

"The same." He laughs. "Coach is totally riding my ass about applying early to Duke, and I'm like, Dude, I don't wanna be stuck in North Carolina for the next four years, no matter *how* good their basketball team is."

"Gotcha."

Then there is silence. The uncomfortable kind.

"I haven't really had a chance to speak with Amy," I tell him. "Her phone always goes straight to voice mail, and she's never around when I call her house. How is she?"

"She's . . . good," Ben says hesitantly. "We've been hanging out a lot since you left."

"Talking about how lost you are without me, I'm sure," I say jokingly.

"You haven't spoken to her at all?"

"For like, five minutes when I first moved, but nothing since. She's impossible to get ahold of. More so than you, even. Is she okay?"

"Yeah, yeah, she's fine," Ben says. His tone makes me

nervous. "Listen, Garrett, there's something you should know. Amy and I . . . well . . . we've kinda been hooking up since you left."

I laugh. It's quick and short, like a hiccup. Then my heart bursts. Suddenly, it all makes sense. Why I haven't heard from Ben until now. Why Amy has avoided me.

Oh God.

"I know it's totally weird, and we didn't plan it or anything. It sort of just happened. I hope you're not upset. I mean, we're over, right?"

I remind myself to breathe. *Don't cry, don't cry, don't cry.* "Right."

"And Amy's your best friend, I get that, but it's not like we're dating. It's just a little bit of fun." Long pause. "Are you mad?"

"Why are you telling me this, Ben? Are you trying to hurt my feelings?"

"Of course not," he says. "I just thought you should know."

So many possible responses rush in and out of my head. "I should go" is what I ultimately choose. "It's late here, and I've got class early in the morning."

"Okay," Ben says. "Sleep well, Garrett."

I think about my list of past boyfriends and the blank space next to Ben's name meant for his last words. Now I have something to fill in: *Sleep well, Garrett.* The last thing he will ever say to me.

Afterward, I am surprised by how much I *feel*. I hide underneath my covers and pour every single emotion I have onto my pillowcase. When I'm done, everything is wet with tears and there is a hollow, empty space inside of me where my feelings for Ben used to hide and where I thought my friendship with Amy still lived.

DUFFY LYRICS RUNNING THROUGH MY HEAD AS I THINK ABOUT HOW BEN AND AMY BETRAYED ME

"It was just my mistake, thinking you cared."
—*Hanging On Too Long*

"My love for you has turned to hate."
—*Delayed Devotion*

"In an instant you were gone." —*I'm Scared*

I'm such an idiot.

I try to wash the redness from my face but it only worsens. I brush my teeth and brush my hair and brush every thought of Ben and Amy as far away from me as possible.

In my room, I can't seem to get comfortable anywhere. I stare longingly at my phone. Who am I supposed to call about this? About discovering that my best friend has betrayed me and my ex-boyfriend has completely moved on. To my best friend. There's always the J Squad, who should be my logical choice. My girlfriends. Of course they'll care, right? I try London's cell phone. No answer. Then I call Jyllian, only it goes straight to voice mail. I'm about to dial Jessica when it hits me, and I have to sigh at the total fucked-up-ness of the fact that the one person who I want to call, who I know can comfort me, who at this point knows me better than anyone else, is the one person whose sympathy I don't deserve. Who I promised myself I didn't want to depend on. Yet, I want—need—to talk to him, to see him. Where does that leave me?

He picks up on the first ring.

"Hey, it's me."

"Hey, you."

"Can I come over?" I ask.

"Is everything okay?"

"No," I tell him. "Not really."

"Yeah, sure. Of course."

"Thanks. I'll see you in a bit."

I get dressed and make myself look as presentable as possible. I pack an overnight bag and tell my parents that I'm staying at London's. They don't ask why I look like I've been hit in the face with a brick. I suppose it's a good thing, because if they knew what just happened and where I'm actually going, they would never let me leave.

HENRY

INT.–MY BEDROOM, SATURDAY NIGHT

"You sure you're okay?"

Garrett nods. Her face is red and I can tell she's lying, but I don't press her. I know how it is to have something on your mind and not feel like sharing.

"So . . . wanna watch a movie or something?" I ask, trying to lighten the mood.

"Okay." Garrett shrugs off her coat and falls onto my bed. I'm sitting with my back propped against the wall;

she rests her head on my leg and looks up at me. "What do you want to watch?"

"I was thinking maybe *Shakespeare in Love*," I say. "You've never seen it, right?"

"But it's so long."

"You rushing off somewhere?"

"No, it's just that we've watched a lot of sappy love stories recently and I'm in the mood for something else."

"Sappy? This is *funny*," I tell her, pointing to the DVD case. She picks it up and turns it over, reading the back.

"I thought it was really serious."

"No way," I say. "I can't believe you've never seen it. Come on. For me?"

She laughs. "Okay."

I get up and fiddle around with my setup; I've watched this movie so many times that it's all scratched up. I blow on the DVD and rub my shirt along the edge. It takes a few minutes but eventually the Main Menu page appears. I settle onto my bed with Garrett.

"Ready," I say. My insides are gooey and my feet are pulsing and my arm is *so* close to hers. We lie just like that, barely touching. I cannot think of anything more incredible than being with her.

Even though I've seen *Shakespeare in Love* before, watching it with Garrett makes it brand-new. It seems fitting that, after viewing the Top Ten romantic movies "of all time" at Huntington Cinemas together, I can share this with her alone. Just the two of us.

The movie is exactly as I remember it. There is comedy and there is drama and most of all there is love, love that pours out of each scene, out of the playhouse, out of Gwyneth Paltrow and Joseph Fiennes—out of every word they say and every way they touch; love for money and fame, love for the theater, but above all, true love. Garrett laughs a lot, which makes me happy.

There's a scene toward the end where everything goes wrong: Joseph Fiennes, who plays Shakespeare, has lost the love of his life, Viola De Lesseps (Gwyneth Paltrow), and he's sure the play he's getting ready to debut, *Romeo and Juliet*, is going to be a disaster because there is no one to play the role of Juliet. But then Viola appears— he didn't know she was at the performance, and she's memorized all the lines because he's recited them to her in bed each night. She enters the stage—at a time when women are forbidden to perform—and he watches her from a few feet away, and he is trembling at how much he loves her, how much he is moved by her. Even though she has just married someone else and will be leaving England for America, and their love can never be realized, it's *real*.

This scene has never truly struck me until now.

When it's over, we are so entwined it's difficult to tell what is hers and what is mine. Her hands have crawled underneath my shirt, our legs are crisscrossed, our feet are touching. Everything is warm. I have never felt closer to another person.

"So, did you like it?" I ask, already knowing the answer.

"I loved it," she says without hesitation.

"*Love* is a pretty strong word."

She moves her body away from mine. I am momentarily upset, but then she is on top of me, staring right at me. "I know."

"There's something I have to tell you," I say.

"What is it?"

"I don't want there to be any secrets between us, okay?"

She looks nervous. "Um, okay."

"Back when we first met, Duke and Nigel assumed we hooked up and, well, I sort of let them think that we did." I wait for a reaction but don't get one. Garrett is completely still. "I don't know if you heard any rumors like that or not—"

"Why would you let them think that?"

"I guess it was easier than explaining that we didn't, and that I maybe had feelings for you, because I didn't really understand my feelings and they scared me. They still do, kind of. I never imagined I would see you again, let alone that you'd be going to East Shore. And once I saw you at school . . . I could have told Duke and Nigel the truth, but I didn't. I don't have a good reason, and I'm sorry." I finish saying all of this and feel incredibly raw. "I'm just really sorry, Garrett."

I'm not sure what to expect. Will she yell at me or smack me or start to cry? Any—or all—of those responses would be acceptable. But she just *looks* at me. What is going on in her head?

"It's okay," she says finally, her voice steady. "I'm glad you told me."

"So you're not mad?" I ask.

"No. I understand."

She puts her hands on my cheeks.

"Hey, blue eyes," I say, staring at her. "God, you're beautiful."

I kiss along her forehead, her eyelids, down her nose, and then her lips, which open to meet mine. My kisses drip onto her neck, her shoulders. I close my eyes and sigh; when I open them her shirt is off and she's pulling mine off too. I unclasp her bra and hold her breasts in my hands, feeling their weight, and take one of her nipples in my mouth. The room is dark except for a muted light in the corner that makes everything glow. It feels like the very first time I have ever felt another person's body above my own. She whispers my name and it's as if I have never heard it before. I am nervous. I am shaking. I am so hard it physically hurts. Each time I touch her, she sizzles.

So this is what it's like to be with someone you love. Someone you care about. I never knew it could be this good.

Something within me screams, *This is it! This is the moment!* It feels right, like what's supposed to happen next, the culmination of these past few weeks, what we've been building toward.

"So," I say between breaths, "here's the big question."

"What?"

I smile. I'm trembling. "Should I get out a condom?"

No response. I have no idea what is hiding behind her eyes.

"What?" I ask.

"I don't think we should," she says.

Oh.

Oh.

I can't tell what she's thinking.

I want to ask: Why not?

I want to ask: WHY NOT?!

I want to ask: Are you not attracted to me? Or is there another reason?

I know that Garrett's not a virgin. She's told me as much. And I understand that sex is special. Reserved for someone you truly care about. Someone you maybe even love. But isn't that exactly what we have? Something special? Something that's maybe, well, love? And if you're going to cross the line between friends and not friends, between watching a movie with your clothes on and taking your clothes *off* and hooking up, why *not* have sex?

It's me. It must be me.

We lie next to each other for a few minutes; I have no idea what to say. I am embarrassed. I am confused. Part of me wants to get up out of bed, get into my car, drive to someplace far, far away and never look back. Another part of me wants to talk about why she doesn't want to sleep with me. A third part of me *doesn't* want to talk about it because I am afraid of the answer.

I am paralyzed with fear. I suddenly feel very naked.

"I guess I ruined the mood," I finally say.

"No," she says. "You didn't."

She slides her body over mine and we start traveling to where we were before, but my heart isn't really in it. I can't stop thinking about why I'm not good enough. About what the problem is. I feel pathetic and disgusting.

About ten minutes later, I ask: "How about now?" It's

sort of lighthearted, but I also hope/wonder/pray that she has changed her mind.

She laughs. "No."

We roll around and mess up the covers and with every kiss I hope that maybe something will be different. "Now?" I ask.

"Nope."

Eventually, I stop trying. We finish and she takes a shower. I stay in my room and wonder what just happened. Why can't I be happy that we spent time together? Why does the fact that we didn't have sex mean that the night was a failure?

Garrett crawls back into bed with me and says goodnight. I try to fall asleep but I can't. I stare at the ceiling and will myself not to cry. We may be in the same bed, but there is an ocean between us. How is it I've never had a problem getting random girls to sleep with me and yet the one girl I have ever really wanted to share myself with turns me down? Why have I attached so much weight to this one physical act?

What does that say about me?

Garrett sneaks out the next morning before my dad wakes up. She says she'll call me.

I bum around for the rest of the afternoon. I sit down at the piano and play through one of Gavin DeGraw's songbooks and go for a run. I toss a ball around with Max in the backyard. I cannot stop thinking about last night.

Maybe it's not a big deal. There are a million reasons why she could have said no. Most of them probably make a lot of sense. After all, I know she was upset about something when she first came over. But all I am convinced of is this: *She doesn't like me. She doesn't want me.*

I have never cared what anyone thought of me before. It never mattered. Now, though, it does, and the idea that two people who are clearly so right for each other can feel so differently about one special act—sex—confuses the hell out of me. Isn't love, in its most basic form, physical? Isn't that what separates the way you feel about a friend from the way you feel about a girlfriend? An emotional connection isn't everything—what about sparks? What about fireworks? What about an explosion?

But explosions are fleeting. I know this from experience. And when they're over, you're not left with all that much. There are girls I've been with whose names I can't even remember. So I guess the difference between hooking up with someone you don't really care about versus hooking up with someone you *do* care about is like the difference between lighting a sparkler in your backyard and Fourth of July fireworks. It's so much better when there's a connection that runs beneath the skin. It's so much better when there's love. Or at least the possibility of love.

I know Garrett feels it. I know she does. So why did she say no?

Around five, Duke and Nigel show up unannounced on my front porch.

ME
Uh, hey, guys. What's up?

DUKE and NIGEL
What's up with you?

They walk past me and deposit themselves at my kitchen table. They look serious.

ME
So?

NIGEL

When were you gonna tell us that Garrett works at

the movie theater with you?

Ouch. I am one hundred percent caught.

ME

How did you guys find out?

DUKE

Some freshman girl saw you two—

NIGEL

(interrupting)

What does it matter <u>how</u> we found out? We found

out. You lied to us.

ME

I didn't lie, technically.

NIGEL

What do you call it, then?

ME

Omitting the truth?

DUKE

You're whipped, man.

NIGEL

Whipped.

ME

What?

NIGEL

We don't want you seeing this girl anymore, Henry.
She's messed with your head. You don't hang out
with us anymore, you don't return our calls, and
now Destiny's Sweet Sixteen is, like, a week away
and we have nothing planned.

DUKE

Nothing. And it's your fault.

They're not wrong. I haven't been hanging out with
them, and Garrett *has* messed with my head. A day ago, I
would have told Duke and Nigel to back off, but after last
night I'm not so sure anymore.

ME

Fine. So I've been hanging out with
Garrett a lot. I'm sorry.

DUKE

Not good enough. We want our old friend back.

NIGEL

This is exactly why we don't hook up with the same
girl more than once. They're like witches. They
hypnotize you.

ME

First of all, you guys don't really hook up with <u>anyone,</u>
so there's that. Second, nobody's hypnotized me,
and Garrett isn't a witch. I hang out with her
because I like her.

NIGEL

You used to like <u>us,</u> too, Henry. We've been friends
for a long, long time, and it sucks to see you throwing
all that away because of some girl—no matter who
she is. We don't deserve to be treated like this.

DUKE

It sucks even more that you're seeing her behind
our backs. And lying about it! We've been there for
you a lot, man, especially . . . you know.

ME

Especially what?

DUKE

After your mom left.

ME

My mother doesn't have anything to do with this.

NIGEL

She has <u>everything</u> to do with this. We know you
haven't had it easy, Henry, but it's not like we're
living perfect lives either. Friends share things, and
they help each other. They don't keep secrets.

I let Nigel's words sink in. He's right, of course. I've
been pushing them away because of Garrett, because of
the feelings for her I don't really understand. Even though
Duke and Nigel mean well, they have no idea what's going
on in my life. Which is my own damn fault.

I look at them with sad eyes. "I'm sorry," I say.

DUKE

Let's all kiss and make up, okay? We have <u>a lot</u> of
work to do for Destiny's big day.

His words hit me like a punch. Planning for a Sweet
Sixteen—even if it *will* be on MTV—is the absolute last
thing I want to do right now. I'm exhausted. Everything
about the night before comes back to me in a flash. I'm
worried about Garrett and sad about myself, and I can't
deal with debating what kind of stupid prank to pull at a
party that doesn't even matter.

ME

You know what? Count me out.

NIGEL

Come again?

ME

I'm out. Not interested. You can mess with Destiny's
party on your own.

DUKE

(like he's about to cry)

You don't really mean that, do you?

ME

I do.

Duke and Nigel look at each other; obviously, they're shocked.

NIGEL

I don't know what's happened to you, buddy, but
something is very, very wrong. And we're gonna do
whatever it takes to get you back to your old self.
Do you hear me? <u>Whatever it takes.</u>

DUKE

P.S., Henry. Screw you.

Duke shakes his head and stomps out of the kitchen. Nigel follows him. This is not good.

Two hours later, I leave my house. Dad's watching TV— I doubt he'll realize I'm gone.

I drive around aimlessly for a while, feeling sorry for

myself. I'm sick over what happened with Garrett. I feel terrible about how I treated Duke and Nigel, who would do anything for me. Eventually, I find myself outside the Jericho Terrace, where I've crashed a fair amount of Sweet Sixteens. It's just getting dark; the entire building glitters with light.

I pull into the parking lot across the street and open my trunk. Inside is a spare suit (plus a shirt, tie, and dress shoes) for emergencies such as this. I don't know if any Sweet Sixteens are happening, but there must be a party I can sneak into. Maybe it'll make me feel better to dance, to get lost in a crowd. That used to make me so happy. Only now I wonder if I was ever really happy, or if I was just fooling myself.

I sneak in through one of the service entrances, navigating the familiar turns until I'm in the lobby. I find the bathroom and go into one of the stalls, take out a flask I filled up with vodka before I left, and swallow. It burns. Then I splash some water on my face and emerge as though I'm just another partygoer.

No one even notices me.

I find myself in one of the larger halls, which is packed with tables and food and people, all in their fancy clothes, grooving on the dance floor. The DJ is loud and the lights are dim. This place is perfect. I have no idea what kind of party it is; everyone looks slightly older than me. Maybe it's a wedding. I close my eyes and start to move. I haven't really eaten anything today, and the alcohol hits me pretty fast.

My feet are moving so quickly I can't feel the ground. I'm starting to sweat through my shirt. I need a break. I blink a few times, searching for a bar, and finally see one in the corner. I want some water to cool me down, to help me think straight.

I ask for a glass with ice and down it in a second. I ask for another, and finish that one too. I'm about to ask for a third when I feel a tap on my shoulder. Busted. I turn around, trying to think of an explanation for why I'm there, and see someone I do *not* expect to see.

LONDON

Henry?

ME

Mmm?

LONDON

What are you doing here?

What is *she* doing here? Maybe she'll just go away.

LONDON (cont.)

Are you okay?

ME

I'm super. Stellar. How are you?

LONDON

I thought you only crashed Sweet Sixteens.

ME

I'm trying to, uh, broaden my horizons.

LONDON

In fact . . . I heard you didn't crash
any parties anymore.

I'm too drunk to figure out what she's implying, but it probably has something to do with Garrett. The last person I want to think about right now.

I shake my head and start to walk away.

ME

See ya.

LONDON

Henry, wait—

She grabs my arm. I wobble for a second and she pulls my other arm, dragging me closer. Her perfume is so strong I have trouble breathing.

LONDON (cont.)
We don't talk anymore, and that makes me sad.
Don't you think it's fate, running into each other
here? I've missed you.

It's not fate. It's a party. And I might cry, because I'm pretty sure that the only girl I've ever really liked doesn't want to be with me.

But I don't say any of those things, and before I realize what's happening London has pressed her lips to mine. I try to pull away but her grip is strong. Also, it doesn't feel half bad.

LONDON (cont.)
I forgot what a good kisser you are.

ME
Listen, London, I can't—

LONDON
Don't be silly. Come on. I know a spot where we
can be . . . alone.

I have to make a decision, only my head is spinning and Garrett has made me feel so undesirable that maybe it wouldn't hurt to spend some time with someone who actually *wants* to be with me, even for just a moment.

Before I have time to stop myself from doing something I know I will regret, she takes my hand. I follow her. I am breaking the Crasher Code. I am breaking the trust I have built with Duke and Nigel. I am breaking the trust I have so quickly yet diligently built with Garrett. But screw it—right now I just don't care.

GARRETT

"You look beautiful," my mother says, running a brush through my hair.

I'm sitting in front of my mirror. Mom hunts through her makeup box and pulls out a tube of mascara. "Are you excited about the party?"

Destiny's Sweet Sixteen. The night the past two months have been leading up to. Excited? No. Terrified? Hell yes.

"I guess," I say.

"I'm looking forward to meeting this mysterious date

of yours," Mom says. My parents have been fishing for details over the past couple of days, and I've given them very little to go on—just a name, really. "Henry."

The mention of his name makes me dizzy. We've barely spoken all week, since the night I slept over at his house but didn't sleep with him. Our conversations have been superficial and weird, both of us skirting around the issue of where, exactly, this relationship is heading. If it even is a relationship. Which it's not. Not really.

I wish I could tell him that I didn't sleep with him because, when he apologized for the rumor, I realized just how he serious he is about me, and how much I really do like him. And with that realization came an incredible amount of sadness. If I follow through with the original plan and break things off at Destiny's party, I will destroy him, and that is no longer what I want. But if I don't, I'll have failed to achieve my own goal: to find happiness and strength *without* a boy in my life (which, truthfully, is a more arduous journey than I expected).

Not to mention, the J Squad will eat me alive.

"So, are you two an official *couple*?" Mom asks as she attempts to lengthen my lashes. "I thought you were swearing off boys until college."

"I am," I say, sighing. "I mean, I was. I mean . . . it's complicated."

Mom laughs. "Relationships are always complicated, Garrett."

"Yeah, but this one is especially murky."

She moves on to the eye shadow, the eyeliner, the lip liner, the lipstick, the blush, and the powder. I usually go for a more natural appearance, but I must admit, the woman's got talent. When I look in the mirror I barely recognize myself.

"Why don't you explain it to me?" Mom asks. "I'm a good listener."

She is, it's true. What am I supposed to say, though? The major reason why I put this plan into motion in the first place was to teach Henry a lesson. Only, it's clear to me that he's already learned one—more than one, maybe. So can I really go ahead with doing what I promised the J Squad I'd do? And now that Henry has been completely honest with me, isn't it my turn to be honest with him?

I lean back on my bed, resting my head against the wall. I want to tell my mother what's been going on, to have conversations like we used to have back in Chicago, before we moved and my life got so "Screwed Up" (Ludacris, 2003). But what will she think of me?

"You know you can tell me anything," Mom says, resting a hand on my shoulder. "What's going on? You can leave out the dirty parts if you want."

I force a smile. "Okay." I take a deep breath and start from the beginning: me and Henry and the J Squad and the bet and Amy and Ben and Destiny's Sweet Sixteen. It sounds more like the plot of a ridiculous teen movie than anyone's actual *life*.

"Wow," she says once I'm finished. "Just . . . wow."

"I know."

My mother looks away, toward the window in my room. I can only imagine what she's thinking, whether she is judging me or not. "Why didn't you tell me any of this before?" she asks.

"Because I knew you wouldn't approve. Besides, using Henry isn't something I'm particularly proud of. Not anymore, at least. I wasn't exactly shouting it from the rooftops."

Mom comes over and sits next to me. "Honey, look. Every strong relationship is built on trust. And it seems like you and Henry have a very shaky foundation."

She's right.

"But really, Garrett, there's only one thing that matters. Do you love him?"

It's not the question I'm expecting—especially from my mother. "What?"

"Henry. All else aside. Do you love him?"

"I mean, I—"

"It's a simple question, Garrett, with a simple answer. Yes or no. Do you love him?"

It *is* a simple question. And even though I never intended to feel this way about him, even though I've tried to fight my feelings and follow through with my initial plan, even though the last thing I want right now is another boyfriend, there is a very simple answer: "Yes."

"Then you have to tell him," she says. "Tell him everything and hope that he forgives you."

"I still don't want to *be* with him, though. He's a great guy and a wonderful friend, but that's it."

Mom challenges me with her eyebrows.

"Oh, fine," I say. "*And* he'd probably be the best boyfriend ever. At another point in time he would have been ideal. But everything I wanted when we moved here—to be alone for once, to figure out who I am—I still want. I'll be eighteen in a few months, and college isn't that far away. It's time to focus on me."

"Then tell him that, too," Mom says. "But *talk* to him. You owe him that much. You're never going to be strong by making someone else weak."

Why did it take my mother to make me see just how flawed this plan was from the get-go? Why did I ever think that hurting Henry would make me feel "Better" (Regina Spektor, 2006)? I could make Henry fall for me and then dump him a million times and it would never erase the scars from my past relationships.

How could I have been so naïve?

Mom leans over and rubs my shoulders. "I didn't mean to upset you, Garrett. You need to make the right decision for you. I'll support you either way."

Just then, I hear honking. I peek through the blinds in my room and see a white stretch limo idling in my driveway.

"That's my ride," I say. "I guess I should go."

"Honey!" my dad calls from downstairs. "They're here!"

I walk carefully downstairs (I cannot afford to fall on my face and accidentally rip this dress) and Mom follows me. Dad is waiting by the front door, camera in hand. Henry is standing there too, in a tux that makes him look more gorgeous than any one person should be allowed to look.

"Picture time!" says Dad. "Come on, Garrett, stand right here next to your boyfriend."

"He's not my boyfriend," I say before I can stop myself. The two of them look at me oddly. I stand next to Henry. He awkwardly slides his arm around me. "Okay. We're ready."

"Erm, smile!" says Dad. "On the count of three. One, two, three!"

We take a few pictures, and Henry gives me a corsage that matches my dress. "Thanks," I say.

"You look . . ."

"Nice?"

"More than nice," he says. "Stunning."

"Well, we should go," I say, waving goodbye to my parents and dragging Henry outside.

"Bye!" Mom yells. "Dance the night away!"

"You really do look beautiful," Henry whispers in my ear. His breath is warm against my neck. I'm tempted to kiss him but I don't.

"Look, there's something I need to talk to you about."

"What is it?" he asks.

Before I can say anything further, London sticks her head out of the sunroof and screams, "Come on!"

"Just a minute," I answer.

"Now! We can't miss the red carpet entrance, and we're already five minutes late!"

I glance at Henry. "I Hate This Part" (the Pussycat Dolls, 2008). Our conversation will have to wait.

The limo is only for the J Squad and their dates (plus me and Henry). Jessica is taking a guy named Frank, who's on the football team at Hofstra, and Jyllian is going with this guy named Aaron, who uses a lot of hair gel. London is going with a Spanish-looking boy I have never met before, who's apparently a sophomore at NYU.

"Garrett, this is Juan," London says with a hand flourish. "Juan, this is Garrett."

"Hola," he says. His hair is long and wavy. *"Eres muy bonita."*

"No, you are!" I say. "I mean, whatever."

"Juan is from Madrid," London says, dabbing her chin with a Neutrogena blotting sheet. "Isn't that romantic?"

"Eres mi princesa," Juan says, giving London a kiss.

She pushes him away and rolls her eyes. "Everyone ready to get this party started?" she asks. "They're not allowed to stock the limo with alcohol because we're under eighteen, but my parents agreed that's *totally* unfair, so they gave me a few bottles of these." She points to what I assume is expensive champagne. "Henry, would you like to do the honor?"

"Uh, sure," he says, looking incredibly uncomfortable. He unwraps the foil on one of the bottles and pops the cork. It shoots across the inside of the limo and everyone laughs. Plastic glasses are passed around; London raises hers to make a toast. "To us!" she says giddily.

"To us!" everyone replies.

I look around with fresh eyes at the girls I have been

trying to impress. Did they ever really like me? Were they actually going to honor their promise? Do I even really care? Is being their friend more important than telling the truth? Than surrounding myself with people who are actually, well, good-hearted?

Really, though, who am I to say who's good and who's not? I thought Amy was good and look at what she did: got with my ex-boyfriend the moment I left town. And I think *I'm* a good person, sure, but look at what I did—what I'm *doing*—to Henry, and for what?

"Garrett," someone says, "you're not drinking."

I stare at the bubbly liquid in my glass. I feel Henry's arm around me. I know I have a serious decision to make tonight. "I'm suddenly not thirsty."

Destiny's Sweet Sixteen is being held in a mansion on the water in Sands Point. It's ridiculously decadent (or, as the J Squad would say, *lavish*). There's a stable and a tennis court and a pool with a waterfall. Halloween is in full effect: there are carved pumpkins with tiny lights inside them that line the driveway. Everything looks gothic and spooky. An actual red carpet is outside the front door; cameramen and photographers are everywhere. The lights are blinding.

"This is intense," Henry says as we exit the limo. He

grabs my hand; his touch startles me. There is so much I have to tell him.

"I feel like I'm in a movie," Jyllian says, taking it all in.

"Really? Because I feel like I'm at Destiny's Sweet Sixteen," London says dryly.

"Well, *I* feel like I'm in a fashion shoot for *Cosmo* or something," Jessica says, reaching into her purse and pulling out a Japanese fan.

Once we reach the carpet, people start taking pictures; I have to admit the whole thing is incredibly surreal. The J Squad make a few funny poses, and I grab Henry's arm and kick my leg up for the goof.

"Listen, Henry, I have to tell you something."

"Yeah," he says, grabbing my hand again. "I have to tell you something too. You wanna go first?"

"Guys," London says, coming up from behind and draping her arms around us. "We *must* see if we can score a drink from the bartender." She turns to Henry. "You're pretty good in that department, aren't you, Arlington?"

"I guess."

"I'm just going to borrow your *boyfriend* here for a hot second," London says, flashing me a grin and pulling Henry inside. Over her shoulder, she yells: "Be right back!"

Ugh.

I stand on the red carpet as people rush past me. Kids from school wave hello and kiss me on the cheek, legitimately happy to see me. Is this what I'll be giving up if I tell Henry why I started hanging out with him in the first place? Will I miss this? But what really is there to miss: a bunch of people who only started paying attention to me once I fell in with the J Squad?

DESTINY'S CHILD LYRICS RUNNING THROUGH MY HEAD WHILE I CONTEMPLATE WHETHER TO TELL THE TRUTH AND RISK LOSING EVERYTHING

"I'm a survivor." —*Survivor*

"I don't think you're ready for this jelly."
—*Bootylicious*

"Nasty, put your clothes on, I told ya."
—*Nasty Girl*

I don't have a coat on, and it's kind of cold. I hear the click of cameras and the voices of people readying for Destiny's entrance (which will, apparently, be via helicopter), but if I close my eyes all I can see is Henry.

Someone taps me on the shoulder. "What are you doing?"

I turn around and Jessica is laughing while her date tickles her. "Nothing," I say.

"Well, come on, then! Let's party!"

"Yeehaw!" Jyllian screams, throwing her arms in the air.

I pray this night doesn't end in complete and irrevocable disaster.

19

HENRY

INT.–DESTINY MONROE'S SWEET SIXTEEN,
SATURDAY NIGHT

There's nothing like being inside a mansion when a television show is being filmed. Every room is filled with white-hot lights and dozens of crew members dressed in black. Cameramen pace back and forth, testing angles and making sure there are clear, well-marked paths between rooms. I imagine I'm on the set of a high-budget feature film (as opposed to reality TV). The thought makes me smile.

London and I walk through what appears to be the living room, where a bunch of people are (dirty) dancing and a DJ is set up in the corner. I've been to enough Sweet Sixteens to know the party doesn't *really* get started until a few hours in. I wonder what kind of crazy prank Duke and Nigel have planned. This is pretty much the first Sweet Sixteen I've been to as myself—no disguise, no lies. A step in a new direction. Now all I have to do is lose London. And come clean to Garrett that the two of us hooked up.

I'd rather gouge out my eyes with a fork. A dull fork. Or even a spork.

We approach the bar, which is humongous.

ME

You know, they probably won't serve you. But I'm pretty sure Duke has a flask on him. It's no mixed drink or anything, but—

LONDON

Oh, Henry, I don't really want a drink.

ME

You don't?

She moves closer. There are people everywhere; I feel as if all eyes are on me. London and I haven't spoken since we hooked up. Truthfully, I was hoping we wouldn't have to.

LONDON

I've been thinking about you all week.

Uh-oh.

ME

You have?

She runs a finger up and down my arm.

LONDON

I never thought anything would happen between us again, but I'm so glad it did.

ME

You are?

LONDON

It's like, destiny or something. Getting back together after all this time.

ME

Look, London, I don't know how to say this, but . . .
we're not getting back together. I mean, we were
never together in the first place, and well—

LONDON

Wait. You don't want to go out with me?

ME

(awkwardly)

No.

LONDON

Then why did you hook up with me?

I don't want to make her feel bad—at least, not any
more than I already have. She deserves to know the truth,
though.

ME

I was drunk, London. It was a moment of weakness.
I guess I thought it would make me feel better
about what happened with Garrett if—

LONDON

Whoa. Take a step back. You hooked up with me
because of <u>Garrett</u>? What does she have to do
with anything?

ME

We're sort of . . . dating. I think. I thought you knew
that—you're, like, her best friend. Last weekend was
a mistake, a one-time thing. I didn't realize you
wanted anything more than that.

LONDON

But . . . you're <u>not</u> dating! She doesn't
even <u>like</u> you!

ME

What? What are you talking about?

LONDON

I can't believe you're doing this to me. You already
hurt me once, Henry. You have some nerve doing it
again. And I am such an idiot for believing you
could change, or that you even <u>wanted</u> to change.

ME

I can change . . . I <u>do</u> want to change. I'm not the
same person I was two years ago, London. I'm not.
I'm sorry if you want something from me that I can't
give you.

She starts to cry, and I have no idea what to do. I feel
terrible, not having considered her feelings, only thinking
about my own. But I really had no idea that she'd want
something serious . . . or that she would ignore Garrett's
feelings so easily.

Not that I'm in a position to throw stones.

London wipes her nose. Maybe it's because her oh-so-
perfect exterior has been compromised, or simply because
I've seen her show actual emotion, or because my experience knowing Garrett has chipped away at my own facade,
but for the first time I don't see her as a character in a
movie who has no depth. I see her as a girl I have treated
incredibly poorly.

I feel awful.

"I really am sorry," I say.

She looks at me with red eyes. "So are you going to tell
Garrett, or should I?"

I know this shouldn't feel like a threat, but it does.

Clearly, the right thing to do is tell Garrett exactly what happened (and why) and hope she'll forgive me. However, I also know that if I tell her I hooked up with London, there's a (very) good possibility I will lose her.

"I have to figure it out," I say.

London laughs. Actually, it's more of a guffaw. "There's not much to figure out, Henry. Either you tell her or I will."

"It's not really your place to say anything, London."

"It's not? I'm her friend."

"I don't know a lot of things, London, but I *do* know you're not her friend. A friend would never hook up with someone who her friend is dating."

"That sentence is so ridiculous I won't even begin to unpack it," she says venomously. "I'm not going to keep this a secret anymore. A week is enough. And she doesn't even know about what happened sophomore year."

London starts to walk off toward where we left Garrett. I instinctively shoot my arm out to block her path.

"Please don't," I say.

London blinks at me like I'm some nearly extinct animal at the Bronx Zoo. The light from the candles in the room bounces off her hair and makes me see spots.

"Don't tell me you have actual *feelings* for this girl," she says. "You're Henry Arlington. You don't have feelings."

London sounds incredibly like Duke and Nigel right now—I hate it when they lecture me, and they're my best friends. I certainly don't need to hear it from her.

I'm about to respond with something obnoxious when suddenly, out of nowhere, I start to cry. I haven't been able to cry for so long, and now, after telling Garrett about my mom, I can't seem to stop. I think about how I betrayed Garrett by hooking up with London and how Garrett will never forgive me, about how I used London to make myself feel better about what happened with Garrett—only now, I feel worse. I'm in love with Garrett and I've ruined everything.

My whole face feels wet. London just stares at me, completely frozen. After a moment or so, her expression softens. "Wow. You do have feelings for her."

"Yeah," I say messily. "I do."

"Let me get this straight: you, Henry Arlington, the king of the random hookup, who is deathly afraid of commitment . . . actually want to be with Garrett? Like, for real? Like . . . you love her?"

"Yeah." There. I said it. *Say it again, Henry.* "I love her."

I can't believe what I just said. Out loud. Is it true? I kind of have no idea what love is, really, but I do know I've never felt about *anyone* the way I feel about Garrett. She's the first person I want to see in the morning and the last person I want to see at night. The first person I've ever talked to for more than five minutes on the phone, who I can tell anything. The first person I've been able to watch ten movies in a row with and *not* get sick of. The first person who has ever understood me, who has ever *tried* to understand me, who I've told about my mom, and who has made me feel like maybe there actually *is* a person out there in the world who's my partner, who gives me joy, who I miss when she's not there, who drives me crazy just *thinking* about her, let alone touching her.

Is that love? And if it's not, what is?

I look around and see Duke and Nigel standing a few feet away.

"I love her!" I scream, pounding my chest like a maniac. "I love Garrett Lennox!"

DUKE
Dude.

NIGEL
Dude.

DUKE
(looking around)
Be quiet! Someone'll hear you.

ME

That's the point! I <u>want</u> people to hear me!

NIGEL

You need to get a grip, Henry. You've
gone totally mental.

"I haven't, though," I say, grabbing Duke by the shoulders and looking at him—*really* looking at him. "I feel more like myself than ever before."

NIGEL

Henry, you've been acting bonkers ever since you
met this girl, and now you're saying you <u>love</u> her?
This is crazy talk!

"Maybe it is, Nigel, but I don't care." My brain is going buck wild. My heart is throbbing. Where is Garrett? I need to find her.

"Wait," London says, grabbing my wrist. "Listen to me." Jyllian and Jessica have sauntered into the room; they approach us warily, as if they can tell something serious is going down.

Nigel and Duke look as confused as I am.

She clears her throat. "It's about Garrett. There's something you should know."

I cannot run fast enough. I blink the tears out of my eyes but can't see where I'm going. There are walls everywhere, surrounding me, blocking me in. There are too many rooms in this house. I push people out of the way. I feel like a stranger in my own body. What am I doing? Where am I going?

I make my way outside just in time: I can hardly breathe. I am sweaty and my hands are shaking. I trip over my own feet. Dozens of kids from school are standing in a semicircle; there are cameras everywhere. I feel like I'm on speed—everything is rushing, everything is racing—but then I see Garrett and I stop. I pull her from the crowd, onto an open patch of grass in front of the party. People start taking our picture; everyone is looking at us strangely but I don't care.

"Is it true?"

"Is what true?" Garrett asks.

"What London said. Am I just a joke to you? A bet?" I am screaming now. I want to rip every single hair from my head. I want to reach inside myself and dig out my heart and hand it over for her to squeeze until it pops. "Is it true?"

Duke and Nigel have materialized out of nowhere. I can see the J Squad pushing their way to the front of the crowd. There are security guards waiting to whisk us away, I'm sure, but no one seems to be making a move. All cameras are on us. I hear some of the crew members yelling at each other and pointing in our direction.

Garrett moves her head. Not left to right, though. Up and down. "Yes," she tells me. That one word hurts like a million bee stings. Like an electric shock. Like an explosion. "It's true."

20

GARRETT

Sometimes, the truth comes out in ways you wish it didn't; all you can do is hope that someday you will be forgiven, that the blemish will be erased from the permanent record known as your soul.

The whole thing goes down like this:

Henry and I, standing, watching each other. Him waiting for the moment I will break and laugh and say this is all one big joke.

But that moment doesn't come. Because this is not a joke. It's real life.

"I'm sorry, Henry," I tell him, and even though I am, it sounds like bullshit. "I tried to tell you earlier but I didn't have the chance."

"When? When did you try and tell me?"

"Before, at my house, and—"

"Tonight doesn't count," he says. "You've been lying to me for weeks. How could you?"

Everyone I go to school with is staring at us. All the people I wanted to like me, I wanted to impress. Henry's face sours and I have to turn away. I can't look at this person I have grown to care about so deeply and not feel like the most wretched, deceitful girl in the entire universe. Even though I never really saw it coming until it was "Too Little, Too Late" (JoJo, 2006). "Honestly."

"You lied to me," Henry says, rocking back and forth. "You acted like you loved me, and I told you things—things I've never told anyone before." He points at London, Jessica, and Jyllian, who are standing diagonal to me. "Did you hang up the phone with me every night and then give them the scoop on how fucked I am?"

"No," I say, reaching out for him. He flinches. "Of course not. Our friendship was real, Henry. The stuff we shared was real. I promise."

Duke and Nigel walk toward Henry, one on either side of

him. "Let's go, man," Duke says, frowning in my direction. "She's not worth it."

"Umm, aren't you forgetting something?" says London. Murmurs rise from the crowd as she burrows into the conversation. "You can't just be the good guy here," she says to Henry. "Aren't you going to reveal *your* little secret for the cameras?"

I look at Henry. "What is she talking about?"

He hesitates for a moment, and then it spills out. "I hooked up with London. Last Sunday."

Last Sunday. Last Sunday was the day after we . . . Oh, right.

My stomach quivers and my eyes begin to tear. Even though I betrayed his trust, I thought I had discovered the real Henry, the Henry who is kind and sensitive and misses his mother and wants to be in a relationship. *That's* why I feel so horrible about having lied to him. But this . . .

I should have known better.

"Well, then I guess I made the right decision the night before, huh?" I say.

"It wasn't like that," Henry says softly.

"It's not the first time we've hooked up either," London tells me. Her tone is venomous and, at the same time, devastated. "Two years ago we sort of had a thing. Didn't we, Henry?"

It all starts clicking into place. That first day at lunch with the J Squad, when London told me that Henry was a heartbreaker, it was *her* heart she was talking about. All the times she seemed uncomfortable when I spoke about growing closer to Henry. The whole idea of teaching him a lesson—this was all for her, really. She tricked me into doing her dirty work.

Henry looks crushed. "Garrett, listen to me. I hooked up with London because—"

I hold up my hand to silence him. I think of Ben and Amy, my former boyfriend and my best friend, who betrayed me and found refuge in each other. Is Henry the new Ben, and London the new Amy?

I don't know whether I'm actually entitled to be this upset, but I am. I hurt Henry—that much is undeniable. My own feelings, though, surprise me. I am jealous. I am furious. I am devastated.

Why am I never enough?

Finally, I say, "Whatever your explanation is, it doesn't matter. You hooked up with London *the same weekend* you were with me. But for your information, the reason I came over to your house that night was because I'd just found out that my ex-boyfriend and my best friend are now an item. I was upset. And the only person I wanted to be with, who I thought would make me feel better, was you."

"I'm sorry," says Henry. I can see in his face that he means it, even though "Sometimes Sorry Is the Wrong Thing to Say" (Ryan Calhoun, 2008). "If I could take back what I did, I would. But you *lied* to me, Garrett. Is the J Squad why you got a job at Huntington in the first place? Do you even like movies, or is my entire life some big joke to you?" His voice cracks. "Which parts of you are real and which parts of you are make-believe?"

I am about to lose my shit and I don't want to be sobbing in front of the cameras. Also, I hear the sound of a helicopter in the distance; we are probably standing in the exact spot where Destiny is going to make her grand entrance. Hence the menacing-looking security guards closing in on us. "I gotta go."

I haven't gotten very far when I see blond hair coming right toward me to attack. Or embrace.

"Are you okay?" Jyllian asks me, pulling me into a hug. "I'm *so* sorry."

"Here," Jessica says, taking a brownie from her purse. "This will make you feel better."

"No thanks," I say. London is standing behind them. I

wait a few seconds to see if she will speak first. She doesn't.

"This is awkward," Jyllian mutters. "Can't you two just kiss and make up?"

"Are you even sorry?" I ask London.

I watch as she thinks. "I am sorry," she says finally. "I thought he wanted me back, but all he wanted was you." The tears start forming; she tries to shake them away, only it's no use.

"I thought you were my friend," I say. "How could you hook up with him when you knew we were together?"

London chokes back a sob. "Do you hear yourself? You weren't *together.* This whole thing was a game. Only you forgot how to play." She looks at Jyllian, then at Jessica. I watch her face go from red to purple, then back to normal. Jyllian hands her a tissue. "If anyone messed up here, it's you, Garrett." She blows her nose. "And this, girls, is *exactly* why we should never date high school boys."

London turns her back to me and walks away. J & J follow.

I'm not perfect. I know that Henry and I weren't officially "together." He wasn't my boyfriend. I flat-out told London I didn't have feelings for him and that the most important thing to me was earning a spot in the J Squad. But no matter how you slice it, that still didn't give her an excuse to do what she did. A real friend would've known better. But the J Squad were never my real friends. I knew that from the start. Only somehow, that knowledge got lost and I thought, maybe, things would all work out.

Well, they didn't.

And I guess that's okay.

I want so much *more* than the J Squad. I still want friends, sure, but not friends who are going to make me pass a test before I can hang out with them—even if they are the most beautiful, influential girls in school. I want friends I have common interests with—excluding sabotage. Being popular, even just for a little while, doesn't really matter. I don't know why I didn't realize this before. It certainly would have saved everyone a lot of trouble.

People don't forget about my scene with Henry—I'm sure it will be all anyone talks about at school on Monday—but after Destiny jumps out of that helicopter and the party truly gets underway, I'm able to slip out unnoticed. I call my dad to pick me up. Then I wait.

It's pitch black outside, but there's candlelight from the

pumpkins that line the driveway, giving off a romantic atmosphere I *would* have found appealing had tonight not sucked hard-core. How many times do you get to hurt someone who cares about you *and* lose your so-called friends, all within fifteen minutes?

I feel completely drained. I feel stupid and like a total bitch, and also disappointed, not so much in London but in Henry. Not that I blame him, but still—it's shocking to know that the two of them hooked up, and even though it hurts my feelings, it reinforces the decision I made *not* to sleep with him and travel further down the road to a relationship that surely would not have ended well. Mine never do. The boy always winds up dumping me or cheating on me or saying something hurtful. It's better we leave it this way, before either of us gets too damaged. We both have a lot of growing up to do. Better to end things before they really even began.

I don't know whether it's because I'm thinking about him or simply because we're at the same party and just had a fight that was captured on camera and witnessed by nearly the entire East Shore student body (and he's looking for me), but I see Henry walking toward me. His head is slightly bent, his shoulders are rounded, and he looks just about as exhausted as I am.

"Hey," he says once he's close.

"Hey."

We look at each other and I almost cry at the sadness of it all. "So," I say.

"So."

"This is weird."

He smiles but doesn't show any teeth. "Yeah."

"I'm not sure what to say," I admit.

"Isn't this the part where you tell me that even though you initially went after me because of a bet, during the time we spent together you realized how much we have in common, and how great I am, and actually fell for me? And then I'm supposed to be sulky for a little while and talk to one of my friends who doesn't even really like you but tells me that I'd be an idiot to let you go, and then I run after you, maybe in the rain or as you're about to board a bus, and I take you in my arms and kiss you and we live happily ever after?"

He looks at me, hopeful, and it kills me. Could he actually think it would be that easy?

"Why are the only happy endings the ones where the couples get together?" I ask. "Can't they just be friends? Can't that be a happy ending too?" I take a few steps closer and kiss him on the cheek. A peace offering.

"I don't think it can, Garrett."

"I see."

"So, this is really it?" he asks gently.

"Yes," I tell him. "At least for now."

He jerks away. "Don't say that."

"Say what?"

"*For now.* I can't handle that. If you don't want to be with me, then I can't have you in my life. At all."

I close my eyes to keep from crying, letting his words sink in.

"I love you, Garrett. You're the only person in my life I have ever loved. It took me seventeen years to find you. There's never going to be anyone else. Please don't do this."

I try to find the right words, if there are any. "You deserve more than what I can give you, Henry. You're sweet and funny and charming and handsome and there are plenty of girls who'll want to be with you if you let them know you. The real you."

"But there's only one girl I want. *You.* All I've ever wanted is you."

"I've never had a connection with anyone in my entire life like I have with you," I say, and it's the truth. "Ben, any of my other ex-boyfriends . . . that was just dating. That's nothing at all like what I feel for you, which is something I have no experience with. You've taught me so much, Henry, about movies and about life. But I've been in relationships before that have ended really badly. All of my relationships, actually, and I need to learn from my mistakes. To focus on myself for a change and figure out what it is that I actually want in life. Before I knew you, I *never* would have admitted I wanted to pursue something in the music industry, and now . . . now it's something I really want to explore."

"You can do that with me," he says. "We can do that together."

"No. We can't," I say, and it pains me. Each word I utter rips a hole in the center of my body that grows bigger and bigger until I'm afraid it will swallow me entirely. "I care about you so much, Henry. You're the last person in the world I want to hurt. But I know myself and I know what I need to do. And that's to *not* be your girlfriend. I understand if you're angry with me. If you don't want to talk to me, we don't have to talk. It's up to you. I'd really like it if we could still be friends."

I wait for him to respond and realize my dad has been sitting patiently in his car a few feet away. "This is me," I say.

Henry looks at me, and his eyes, which have always been so full—of mystery, of life—seem dull and flat. "Go," he says, his voice trembling. "Just go."

The ride home with Dad is completely silent.

After a while, he says, "You okay, honey?"

I let loose. All of it comes out—tears, snot, more tears—and I just cry.

Dad pulls over to the side of the road. He squeezes my arm and waits until I've exhausted myself. Once I'm done, I look up and he is smiling.

"Boy trouble?"

I laugh. "Yeah," I say, "you could say that."

"What happened?"

"I hurt someone . . . someone I really care about. And I don't know how to make it better."

Dad reaches over and brushes some of my hair back. "That's pretty deep stuff, Garrett."

"I know."

"Well, listen. What I'll say is this: love is hard. For everyone."

"Not you and Mom," I say. "You guys have the perfect relationship."

"Sweetie, no relationship is perfect. There are always ups and downs." He kisses my forehead. "I know things seem rough now, but sleep on it. Time heals everything—corny, but true. And matters of the heart are always sunnier in the morning."

At home, I fall into bed without taking off my dress. All I want to do is text Henry, or call, but I don't. It wouldn't be fair. I curl into a ball and hold my legs.

That look on his face!

I've lost him forever.

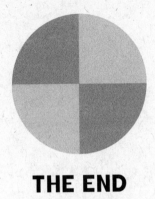

THE END

There is nothing sadder in this life than to watch someone you love walk away after they have left you. To watch the distance between your two bodies expand until there is nothing left but empty space . . . and silence.

—from *Someone Like You* (2001)

HENRY

Relationships take time. They are days and nights and weeks. They are stretched and worked and kneaded into something you never imagined they could be. But when they are over, the end comes so quickly you barely have time to breathe, to blink. They are minutes and seconds, and one moment you have everything and the next you have nothing. So here's my question: when you lose the most important person to you in the entire world, where is all the love—love you never even knew you were capable of—supposed to go?

GARRETT

To: Amy Goldstein<Amy.Goldstein@gmail.com>
Subject: Hey . . .

Truthfully?

I was hoping I'd hear from you by now. I can
only assume you're uncomfortable talking to
me because of this thing with Ben, and I hate
that our friendship was so fragile that a guy
was able to come between us. It hurts to know

the two of you are hooking up. It hurts even more that I heard it from Ben and not from you.

The funny thing is that if I'd found out about this a month ago, it would have devastated me. You were my very best friend in the entire world. But I met someone who kind of changed my life . . . and it's a long story that's not worth telling—or rather, it is worth telling, but not in an e-mail, and maybe, at this point, not to you—and now I'm just sort of thinking about bigger things than you & Ben.

So, I guess the point of this note is to tell you that I forgive you, even though you haven't apologized. I'm taking some time to "find myself" (how clichéd is that?), and maybe we can try this whole friend thing again in the future. If not, it was a good run while it lasted, wasn't it?

I'll have my people call your people.

xoxo,

G

HENRY

It's really over.

I don't go into work during the weekend. I fill my time with nonsense. I eat dinner alone and try to write a song on the guitar (key word: *try*) and check my e-mail. I don't go on AIM. What if Garrett's on?

She wants to be friends. But what does that mean? Were we ever really *friends*? Friends don't stay up talking on the phone Every Single Night about Stupid Little Things and Most Important Things until it's light outside. Friends don't tell each other their most secret secrets.

Friends don't hook up.

Friends don't *ache* for each other.

They just don't.

And when two people share those things, how can one of them simply shut off all the feelings? Is there a switch, a button I don't know about? Is it possible to bypass the pain and hurt, the *what if*s and *maybe*s and *why not*s and *what the fuck*s?

But maybe Garrett never felt that way about me. Maybe she never *ached* for me. I thought she did, but I could be wrong. And does it even matter? I don't know if she felt the same way that I did, that I *do,* but surely she felt something. She must have. You can't fake a connection— that much I know.

I guess she just didn't feel *enough.*

So Garrett was never really my girlfriend and she was never really my friend. I can accept that. Only why, then, am I hurting so much? I barely know this girl. She's been in my life a very short amount of time. Shit, though, did it mean a lot. Why does she occupy every second?

How can you so desperately miss something you never had in the first place?

Ben, all of my ex-boyfriends . . . that was just dating. That's nothing at all like what I feel for you, which is something I have no experience with. Was she lying? I don't think so, but if that's true, then how can you throw it all away? Why aren't I good enough to add to her list of previous boyfriends? What was so great about them?

But I've been in relationships before that have ended really badly. All of my relationships, actually. Doesn't every relationship end badly until you find The One? And how could things possibly end worse than this: me feeling broken and used, the two of us not speaking.

What if we've lost each other forever?

I replay our last conversation like a scene in a film I'm obsessed with. I wonder if someday she will ever want me. But here's the thing: when you press Rewind and start again, all you're doing is seeing the same thing over and over and over. It never changes. I can think about all the things Garrett said to me, and her previous boyfriends, and what I *wish* could happen between us, or I could draft a million e-mails begging her to change her mind, or send her a text, or even pick up the phone and call, but none of that alters the essential ingredient in the recipe of whatever these past few weeks have been. *I want her.* I want her so badly it's maddening, I want her so badly I can taste her and smell her and see her with my eyes closed. But she doesn't want me—at least, not like I want her.

I must accept this.

I must move on.

I make a list of things I need to do and chant them to myself like a personal mantra. A list of goals and where I want to be emotionally a month from now, six months from now, a year from now. I have never really thought about stuff like this. I have never really been this vulnerable.

INT.–EAST SHORE HIGH SCHOOL, WEDNESDAY

Girls in movies (and in high school) forever talk about getting their hearts broken. I've always felt that phrase is incredibly stupid. A heart cannot break. It's muscle and flesh and arteries and veins. And yet, now, I get it. I completely understand.

My heart is broken.

I'm not sure it will ever be the same—like a vase or a ceramic figurine you drop and then glue back together. It may still be functional, but it's no longer beautiful. You can see all the cracks.

I take a few days off from school. When I return, the entire place is different. I barely recognize anything. That's not to say that anything has actually changed—same lockers, same hallways, same random freshmen, same douchey teachers—but, it seems, *I* have changed.

Before Garrett, I walked the halls like I was in a movie. Like I was living someone else's life. I saw people, but I never really *saw* them. I just sort of watched them go by. But now, after Garrett, I see them; they come at me from every direction; they rush past me and bump into me and knock me around. Each time someone brushes my shoulder *I feel it.* Each time someone says my name *I hear it.* It's completely disturbing. It's like I've been living my entire life in black-and-white and finally someone has turned on all the color at once.

"Earth to Henry!"

I turn around. It's Duke.

DUKE

Good to see you've finally resurfaced.

"Yeah," I say. "I guess."

I stare at Duke. He's the same as always, of course, but also so different. Or maybe it's just that *I'm* different.

"You get my messages?" he asks.

"I did. Thanks."

He puts a hand on my shoulder. "So, how are you? Holding up okay?"

"I've been better."

"You're gonna be just fine," he assures me, leading me down the senior hallway and toward the back entrance of the school.

"Where are we going?"

"Out for lunch. Nigel's getting his car. We thought it'd be good for you to . . . ya know . . . not be in the cafeteria on your first day back."

I'm glad. I can just imagine how awful it would be to sit around a table and hear people whispering about me and my so-called tragic breakup (i.e., pretty much how all of my morning classes went).

"Thanks, man," I say.

"No problemo. That's what friends are for."

Duke and me order burgers and fries and a soda at Wendy's. Nigel gets a salad. "I'm watching my figure," he says, patting his stomach.

We mess around and eat and I almost feel . . . normal. Well, *normal* isn't the right word. But I feel okay. Recently, Garrett was my entire life; I completely ignored Duke and Nigel. Even though my relationship with them is in no way comparable to my relationship with Garrett, it feels good to know there are still people who care about me. Who enjoy my company and want to see me happy.

What we talk about: the song Destiny was lip-synching to when one of her boobs accidentally popped out of her dress and the color of the BMW convertible her parents bought her for her birthday (even though she doesn't even have a permit yet).

"So, what'd the big prank end up being?" I ask.

Duke shrugs. "No prank."

"Why not?" I ask. "You guys were so psyched about it."

"We, uh, couldn't do one without you," Nigel says sheepishly. "It wouldn't have been the same."

I'm touched. I owe these guys so much. I don't even know where to begin.

"Also, we couldn't think of anything good," Duke says, laughing.

Finally, the inevitable topic comes up. We have a few minutes before we need to get back to school for sixth period.

"Have you spoken to her at all?" Nigel asks.

"Dude," Duke says, "let it be."

"It's okay," I tell them. "I haven't. She wants to be friends but I just . . . I don't think I can do it."

"Why would anyone want to be *friends* with a *girl*?" Duke asks. Then he goes to high-five Nigel, but Nigel just shoots him a look that says *You are a complete moron.*

"I wish I could be friends with her," I say. "I want her in my life so badly, but . . . as much more than a friend. So much more. And I don't think I can handle anything less. I'm really sorry I shut you guys out." I look at Duke, then Nigel. "You were both there for me when my mom left, and I couldn't have survived without you. Really. I should have been honest with you about Garrett from the start. I don't deserve friends like you guys."

"Yeah, man, you do," Duke says. "We love you, Henry. We just want to see you happy. It sucked you didn't tell us what was happening because we couldn't help you. But now we can."

"Not to get all sappy on your asses," Nigel says, "but my dad has this saying that's like, 'In matters of love and living situations, you've gotta put yourself first.' If you don't think you can handle being friends with her, then don't."

"But I'm really worried about her—"

"Dude," says Duke, "you've gotta worry about *yourself*. Not her. She's a bitch."

"She's not a bitch," I say.

"It doesn't matter if she is or she isn't," Nigel says. "She hurt you, and you need to heal. And that's going to take time. So take all the time you need."

"Or you could just get a random sophomore to give you

an HJ," Duke says, leaning back in his chair. "That always makes me feel better."

Nigel punches his arm, and I laugh, knowing that the only time that has ever happened for Duke is in his dreams.

"And you know," Nigel continues, "even though you probably feel like complete shit . . . there's something, I dunno . . . *alive* about you today. You seem like you're really here with us, you know? Not a million miles away thinking about some random movie you watched last night on IFC. You're gonna be just fine."

Alive. I like that. I do feel alive. I feel like I've been asleep for a million years and I'm finally awake. I am finally ready. For what? I have no freaking clue. But I know that I can never go back to the old me. I can never go back to crashing Sweet Sixteens and hooking up with girls who mean nothing to me. Sex and intimacy, I've learned, are not mutually exclusive. I want a connection. I want romance. I want, I don't know, *love.*

And now that I know what it is to love someone, I want to know what it is to have that love returned. Garrett supplied me with a taste, but that's all it was. A hint. A start. And if I've gained anything from having her in my life, it's realizing that I have a fucking lot to give. The fact that I don't have my mother anymore, and I don't have Garrett anymore, doesn't mean I'm going to die. It means I'm going to live. I have to, really. I've got no other choice.

One night, a few weeks ago, I was talking to Garrett on the phone (it was probably around one or two in the morning) and she was saying something about her dad and I made a comment about my own, and what she said was this: "You're both hurting and you need each other. If he's not going to reach out to you, then you have to reach out to him. You have to push him. It will be hard but I *promise* you that eventually it will all work out."

At the time, I thought it was kind of bullshitty advice. Why should I be the one to go to him? He's the adult. If he wants to run away and sulk every time I even try to mention my mother, that's his problem.

It's not just his problem, though, which I guess is what Garrett was trying to say. It's *our* problem. I only have a year left—less than a year, actually—before I move out of the house and go to college. Sure, I'll be back on breaks and stuff, but it won't be the same. Even though I'm dying to get out of Long Island, I don't want to leave and have things still be so shitty; I don't want to feel like I have no idea who my father really is or like he has no clue about me.

Here's what I know: I swore I'd never fall in love but I did. And it has messed me up and who knows when I'll actually recover. It could be days, it could be weeks, it could be months—or maybe I'll be thirty and still reminiscing about the time I shared with Garrett Lennox. Maybe not. What *has* been revealed, though, is that I have the possibility to change, to become whole, when for so long I have felt so half. Everything until now has been a test, and I have crashed and I have burned and I am weak, but I will come out stronger. I don't have to live my entire life hiding behind a computer or a television or a movie screen. I can step in front of one. And I know just where to start.

I go downstairs to where my father is sitting on the living room couch, watching a college basketball game on the flat screen.

"Dad," I say.

DAD
What's up?

"Not much." I grab the remote and shut off the TV. I take a long, deep breath. "We need to talk."

He looks at me with weary eyes. He sees me. Then he pats the empty spot on the sofa next to him. "Okay."

GARRETT

This is officially the swiftest my life has ever come
"Full Circle" (Miley Cyrus, 2008).

I feel like it's my first day at East Shore all over again,
only worse. Then, no one really paid me any attention.
Now, I'm definitely getting attention, but not the kind anybody wants. Some people, I think, are impressed that I
was the first girl to really crack Henry Arlington. It's important to remember, though, that Henry is as popular as
you can be at East Shore; most people—the girls, at
least—are pissed at me for breaking his heart. The guys

don't want anything to do with me for fear of being ostracized by Duke and Nigel, the leaders of the Hate on Garrett parade. I can't really blame them. Only, I wish someone would understand this isn't easy for me, either.

When you break up with someone, there is, for the most part, a winner and a loser. The winner is the one who initiates the breakup, who's already moved on or has confronted his or her feelings. The loser is the one who is sideswiped, who has no control over the fact that something that once seemed so stable has been decimated.

But anyone who has ever dumped someone knows that it sucks for the winner, too, and really the winner hasn't won anything at all—the only accomplishment is having hurt someone's feelings. Which sucks no matter how it happens.

I hate that I hurt Henry. I hate myself for lying to him and for letting the charade go on as long as it did. I hate myself for developing actual feelings for him and for being unable to express them properly and make him understand that I really do care about him, that I have never known anyone like him before, and that I doubt I ever will.

But I don't hate myself for ultimately being honest. I don't hate myself for trying (and failing) to make girlfriends for once in my life, for putting my own feelings before a boy's, for trying to have some semblance of independence.

When I first moved to Long Island, I thought that if I could make a guy understand what it's like to be dumped, I would feel better about myself. But I've learned that hurting someone doesn't make you strong. And hurting someone I care about feels worse than anything I've ever suffered. It was foolish to think that toying with Henry's emotions would ever provide me with validation, or that hanging out with the J Squad and *pretending* they were my friends would actually turn them into people I'd want to be friends with.

I still have a lot to learn, it seems. But I am ready to start.

The J Squad officially reject me from their cafeteria table.

London approaches me at my locker. "Just so you know," she says, "you can't sit with us at lunch."

"I wasn't exactly planning on it. Where are Jyllian and Jessica—did they send you to be the official bearer of bad news?"

"Jyllian has a physics test and Jessica is scared of you. She's totally having diarrhea in the bathroom right now. And just so you know, you didn't win the bet."

At this point, I don't even care. I know enough to see that London is putting on her brave face and that, inside, she's still reeling from Henry's rejection. If asserting power over me makes her feel better, whatever. I don't need the J Squad.

"If you say so," I tell her.

"Now's the time we *would* make your life a living hell, but judging from the gossip I've heard, you've already done a fantastic job of that yourself," she says. "I just can't wait until MTV airs the episode of Destiny's party in a few months so the *entire country* can see what a skank you are."

There are a few choice responses I think of immediately, but I'm not really in the mood to fight, especially not with London. I close my locker and give her a "Smile" (Lily Allen, 2006). "There's toilet paper stuck to your shoe," I tell her, and then I walk toward the cafeteria to find a table for one.

En route, I see Henry—it's the first time I've seen him since the party. He did send me an e-mail afterward. The subject said "Friends . . ." and underneath he wrote: "I wish I could, but I can't."

I didn't respond.

It's pretty clear that he's avoiding me. I don't exactly blame him, but I wish things were different. But you can wish and you can pray and at the end of the day, that doesn't really change anything. I stand still and watch him pass. He sees me, that much I'm sure of. I give a tiny wave, but he doesn't return it. I think I see a smile, a tight-lipped one, but it may just be the light. I'm too far away to tell. Whatever his expression is, he walks away to somewhere I am not invited.

It's devastating to lose a friend. I wouldn't wish it on my fiercest enemy. I wouldn't wish it on the worst person in the entire world. There is nothing like having everything and then having nothing—no matter how it happened— and longing for that person but being rewarded only by memories that play out like scenes in a movie until you can barely recall what is real and what is not, what is life and what is fiction.

I finally reach the cafeteria. I expect the entire room to stop when I enter, but it doesn't. I maneuver through the crowded room until I find a dingy table that is completely empty. Four or five chairs surround it; I put my books on one, sit on another, and take out my lunch. I debate picking up one of the books and reading, or pretending to read so I don't look so lonely, but screw that—I *am* lonely. I might as well embrace it.

The J Squad are gathered at the other end of the cafeteria,

and I avoid eye contact completely. A few minutes go by. I'm staring at the wall to my left when I hear a voice I don't recognize.

"Hey, Garrett."

I look up. Two seniors are standing in front of me: Melody Brickman and Josie Ramirez. I know them peripherally; they don't socially orbit the J Squad, but they're not complete losers, either. They're just normal, regular girls with normal, regular-looking paper bag lunches of their own.

"Hi," I say. My voice cracks and I take a sip of water.

"We don't want to pry or anything," Josie says, "but we were at Destiny's Sweet Sixteen."

Ah. A few people have come up to me since then, asking me for details about Henry ("Does he have any tattoos? Is it true he hooked up with one of the Pussycat Dolls? Does he use a lot of tongue when he frenches?"); these girls probably want in on the secrets too.

I sigh. "He doesn't have any tattoos but he's not opposed to getting one if he can figure out a meaningful design, he didn't hook up with one of the Pussycat Dolls, although I'm sure he could if he wanted to, and he's a great kisser. Anything else?"

They look at me like I've just escaped from a loony bin.

"Um, what?" Melody asks.

"Henry. That's why you're coming over to talk to me, right?"

Josie frowns. "Not exactly. We just wanted to say that we saw what happened, and we're sorry. If you want to talk about it with anyone, I mean . . . I know we're not really friends, but I'd be happy to lend a shoulder to cry on."

"Ditto," Melody says.

I'm kind of shocked. "I don't really know what to say." I look around for cameras to see if someone is filming our interaction (it wouldn't be the first time), but I don't see any.

"I broke up with my boyfriend over the summer and it was awful. I feel your pain," Melody says. "He still won't talk to me."

"Guys are crazy," Josie says, stifling a laugh.

I smile and a sort of warmth fills my stomach. A tiny ball of hope. "Do you guys want to sit down?"

"Is that okay?" Melody asks. "We weren't sure if you were eating alone or if you just have a lot of imaginary friends."

"Oh," I say, shrugging, "I do, but they don't leave the house. Except on weekends."

We all laugh. Then they sit.

INGRID MICHAELSON LYRICS RUNNING THROUGH MY HEAD AT THE POSSIBILITY OF MAKING NEW FRIENDS

"I just wanna be okay." —*Be OK*

"I am giving up on half-empty glasses."
—*Giving Up*

"I think I'm starting to feel something good."
—*Oh What a Day*

"Thanks," I say.

"For what?" Josie asks.

"Oh." I take a bite of my sandwich and feel some of the weight on my shoulders dissolve. "You know."

At the end of *Shakespeare in Love*, there's a moment when you wonder whether Gwyneth Paltrow's character, Viola, will stay in England with Shakespeare, who she loves, or if she will travel to Virginia with Lord Wessex, who she was forced to marry.

"How is this to end?" Lord Wessex asks the Queen. To which the Queen replies, "As stories must when love's denied: with tears and a journey."

This part of the movie is particularly wrenching—even though Shakespeare and Viola are devastatingly *right* for each other, even though they have a love most people would kill for, a love most people never know their entire lives, it's simply not meant to be.

But unlike Romeo and Juliet, Shakespeare and Viola will not suffer tragic deaths. (This is assuming they are real people as opposed to film characters, but stay with me.) There will be heartbreak, yes, but they will live. There will be tears and there will be a journey. They will go on to have full lives and do wonderful, exciting things. Henry and I will too. I'm sure of it. Because love, no matter how tragic (or rusty, as the J Squad would say), is not an ending. It is a test and a textbook; it is a map to undiscovered places and a lexicon of languages yet to be spoken.

Love.

Really, it is a beginning.

Acknowledgments

Thanks to:

Everyone at Random House Children's Books, especially Krista Vitola, Marci Senders, Kathy Dunn, and Beverly Horowitz. Also to Jillian Karger and Colleen Fellingham for their keen eyes.

My editor, Stephanie Elliott, for her wisdom, wit, and warmth—plus making sure I stay (semi) appropriate.

My family, for their love and support.

Lastly, to the friends who Virgiled me through my own CTL: thank you for helping me realize that it's better to feel everything than nothing at all.

CONTINUE READING
FOR AN EXCERPT FROM
The Diamonds

Excerpt copyright © 2009 by Ted Michael
Published by Delacorte Press
an imprint of Random House Children's Books
a division of Random House, Inc.
New York

The light flicked on, and I was blinded by my nakedness, and his nakedness. The door flew open. Before I could move (there was no time to do anything but freeze), a sea of faces stared down at me—Duncan's, Priya's, Lili's, Ryan's, faces I had never seen before, shocked faces—and in the center of them all was Clarissa's, eyebrows arched in surprise, mouth pulled together in a tiny O that said a million things and nothing at once.

And I remember thinking: *My life is over.*

* * *

The next day, nobody returned my calls.

When I stopped by each one of the Diamonds' houses on Sunday afternoon, they were conspicuously "unavailable." I even went to our regular brunch at Bistro, but they were nowhere to be found. By Monday morning, what had happened at Ryan's party was all over school. For discretionary reasons, I won't repeat the gossip here, but know that it was awful, and that by third period, the entire school was under the belief that there was a sex tape of me, Anderson, and a live chicken floating around the Internet.

AP Lit with the twins was the worst.

"I heard she has 'I heart Anderson' tattooed across her back," Dana said while Mrs. Bloom drew stick figures of Romeo and Juliet on the board. "And underneath that, 'I heart balls.'"

"*I* heard that Lili and Priya never even liked her," said Dara, "and the *real* reason Jed dumped her is because she has warts. Not the kind on your feet, either."

The Diamonds weren't at lunch; they didn't show up for government, either.

Nobody was outright rude to me, but everyone stayed far, far away. The only human contact I had that entire day was two seconds with Anderson after art class, when he whispered, "Call me later, it's gonna be okay," into my ear and fled down the hallway before I could follow.

* * *

After school, Duncan was waiting for me at my locker with an incredibly peculiar expression on his face.

"Hi, Duncan," I started, "I'm really—"

He held up his hand. "Whatever, Marni. I'm just here to give you this."

Duncan handed me a thin slip of paper, which I immediately recognized (I'd helped design them, and conceived the entire text): it was a subpoena, the kind the Diamonds slipped into peoples' lockers if they were supposed to appear at a trial.

"It's for today," he said, leaving before I could reply.

That was okay. I didn't feel much like talking.

There were more people in the chorus room for my trial than for all the previous ones combined. People were clumped around the doorway, balancing on their toes to see inside. To see me.

Clarissa, Priya, and Lili looked formidable and gorgeous in their chic black robes; I thought about mine lying in its garment bag somewhere, and about how—now more than ever—all I wanted to do was put it on and stand beside them.

Members of the jury scowled at me. Neither Mr. Townsen nor Principal Newman was anywhere to be found. Only the

Diamonds and me, separated by a judges' bench and an apology.

Clarissa looked stone cold. "You are being charged with multiple offenses, Ms. Valentine, including First-Degree Backstabbing with Intention to Hurt, Second-Degree Being a Huge Slut, and Third-Degree Fugliness. How do you plead?"

Despite everything, I couldn't help laughing at the ridiculousness of the entire scenario. "Is this for real?"

"We need your answer," Priya said.

"Why didn't you return any of my calls?" I asked.

"Please note that the defendant refuses to answer the question," Clarissa said stiffly, "which automatically enters a default plea of guilty."

I could tell I needed a better tactic. "Look, I have absolutely no desire to talk about this with you guys in front of all these people"—I glanced around the room—"but you're making it impossible to do otherwise, so here goes: I'm sorry." I locked eyes with Clarissa. "This thing with Anderson just . . . happened. I didn't tell you because I didn't want you to be upset. I don't want to lose your friendship over something like this."

For a moment Clarissa's face softened, but then she said, "So you admit to having a secret relationship with Anderson behind my back, and behind Priya's and Lili's, too?"

I felt my heart fold itself in half. "Yes," I said, because

really, what else was there to say? Someone behind me whispered, "Slut," and someone else whispered, "Dumb tranny," which I hoped wasn't about me (but probably was), and before I knew it, Clarissa slammed down her gavel and said, "The Diamond Court finds you guilty of all the above charges." Apparently, she didn't even need to check in with the jury for this one. "You betrayed our trust and you're never to speak to us again. If you see us in the hall, look the other way. Delete our numbers from your phone, and forget our e-mail addresses. Don't sit next to us in class." She leaned forward and scowled. "From this moment on, Marni, you no longer exist."

I was speechless. Lili stepped down from the bench and walked toward me. She looked the same as always, only there was something meaner, something crueler, that lay just beneath her skin. "Hand over your necklace, Marni."

My hand involuntarily went to my collarbone, where my diamond pendant lay against the base of my throat. "You can't be serious," I said, waiting for her to apologize for this outrageous scenario.

"Give us the necklace," Lili said. "Now."

Slowly, I reached behind me and unclasped the one tangible item that proved I was a Diamond, the daily reminder of who my friends were and what my place at Bennington was.

I dropped it into Lili's hand and held on to her fingers before letting go.

"Case closed," Clarissa declared.